HARD TO LOVE

W WINTERS

She was too good for this world. I was too
much of a bastard to push her away.

I grew up in this life, and now I run these streets.
Blood and violence taint everything I touch.

Everything but her. She was my constant through it all.

Just a touch would singe and soothe.

Just a look would tempt and torment.

She became my escape and my addiction.

I only survived because she was by my side.

I should've known better than to indulge.

I should've known better than to let her fall for me.

It was only a matter of time before the danger
bled into what we had.

I was Laura's downfall. Problem was, she was mine too.

HARD TO
LOVE

PROLOGUE

Seth
On the west coast and several years before meeting the Cross brothers.

THIS HOUR OF NIGHT, THE FLOOR-TO-CEILING windows reveal nothing but black outside. Pitch black. Inside, though, the lights shine brightly and keep everyone in this place invigorated. The bass of the music thrums in my veins just as it lightly vibrates the hardwood floors beneath my polished oxfords.

Wrapping my hand around the steel rail that runs along the second-floor loft, with my office behind me, I watch the bright blue lights fade to nearly black in time with the beat. Bodies sway, drinks are poured, and life moves on.

My bar is the hottest spot in all of Tremont. The women, the money, all the shit that goes down in the back rooms—it's all mine. Everyone wants in those black glass double doors. Thank fuck for that. It took nearly a year to get my name back, to get the money, both dirty and clean, flowing easily without someone wanting me dead along the way.

A year of recovering from the damage that was done. A year without her.

A year cleaning up the mess and taking care of shit that nearly broke me. Between all the fights and all the drugs, none of it compares to what happened last year. Two days until the date.

A gruff exhale leaves me as I force away the memories and focus on what's in front of me. The perfect location, the perfect setup. The perfect fucking life I've been building.

The name of the bar mirrors every inch of what's inside. *Allure*. It's designed to lure in customers and to keep the drinks flowing, the hips moving, and the money streaming in. The bar is seductive with polished black marble waterfall counters that gleam, their shine visible from all the way up here. The deep cobalt velvet sofas on opposite sides of the seating area are just as enticing as the women who perch themselves there with crystal glasses containing pink cocktails in their manicured hands as they let out peals of feminine laughter. Black crystal chandeliers drip from the ceilings.

Club Allure is about escaping from reality via luxury and illusions of grandeur.

The basement though... and the back rooms... those are the real moneymakers, all of it under the table, and how I earned the fear and respect that comes with my name.

It's also what led to enemies. You haven't made it in

this world until someone tries to take what's yours. Until someone wants to challenge you. Until someone wants you dead.

I learned that hard lesson a year ago. And the ones who came for me? Their deaths didn't go unnoticed by anyone else who thought they could take from me.

An eerie prick travels down my spine as my mind wanders to places in the past. Back to when I was a different man. Things change when the ones you love the most leave you. Just as I think about everything that happened before this, just as the memories invade the present, I swear I hear her voice.

It's only a memory. *She's only a memory.* I remind myself like I've done so many silent nights, only to have my gaze drawn to the sound again.

The crowd doesn't part for her; she blends into it, which is what she always wanted.

I see her though, and everyone else blurs as I focus on her alone.

My grip tightens on the rail and everything pauses around me. My blood runs scorching hot. Her dark brunette hair cascades down to her lower back. In distressed dark denim shorts and a silk cream tank top that hangs low on her back, she makes her way straight to the bar. I watch as the corners of her lips turn up at recognizing the two men behind the bar. They've been my crew since the first day... she was there too.

She was always there, always a part of us.

Connor sees her first, dropping the empty glass he's

holding on the counter to reach across the bar. When he calls out, "Babygirl," Roman looks up from the set of four shots he's pouring and grins at her.

It's too loud on this floor to make out everything they're saying. It's all smiles and hugs, though. Warm, friendly greetings. It steals any heat I had and leaves a chill to settle over my shoulders, slowly wrapping its way around me as the time ticks away.

The two of them barely let her get a word in as they talk, but she laughs—fuck, I can hear that sweet mirth all the way up here. Just like I can see the rosy flush in her cheeks when she agrees to take a shot with them. Just like I can see the dip in her throat that I used to lick when she throws back the shot of clear liquid.

It's been a year, but I swear I remember the way she tastes.

It takes a minute before she asks them something. She rocks on her heels as she waits for an answer and both of the guys look around the first floor.

It's when they point to Derrick that the hate creeps in. That chill on my skin turns to ice and I decide I'm sick of waiting.

She asked for Derrick. Not me.

My eyes are trained on her as I make my way down the stairs. My jaw is set as it is, and I can't change that fact for the world right now. Past the masses dancing on the floor, I make my way easily to where Derrick's seated in a leather wingback chair on the far edge of the wall where security is located.

A woman turns around, tall and slim, when I brush past her. I barely notice anything about her except the short red dress that clings to her curves. She smiles when she sees it's me, her eyes hopeful but she quickly lowers her gaze and backs away.

Maybe it's the hate in my glare that told her I'm not in the mood for these games tonight.

I'm barely contained, hardly capable of a single rational thought as that last moment I had with Laura runs through my mind. The past and the present swirl in front of me, hitting me harder and more forcefully than the strongest cocktail I could drown myself in.

Laura plants a kiss on Derrick's cheek… It's short lived and her smile is sorrowful.

The anger that carved itself into a glower relents and dims. Even a year isn't enough time. There will never be enough time passed to make it better.

Regret is my enemy. Guilt its friend.

I'm standing there like a lion stalking his prey when Laura turns around, not looking where she's going, brushing stray strands of hair from her face as she bumps right into me.

"Sorry," she quickly breathes, and then she looks at me. Her blue eyes have flecks of gold in them, and like a concoction of emotion they swirl as she stares at me. Her lips are slightly parted, and they stay like that. Open and waiting with disbelief.

"Laura." I say her name and feel the thrill of doing just that simmer in my blood.

"Seth," she whispers. Her shoulders drop slightly and then she covers herself, as if instantly cold.

"I um, I had something to give Derrick," she tells me, but her eyes don't stay on me. They stray, unable to keep my gaze. I watch the cords in her neck tighten as she swallows; I can't help but notice how her hands keep nervously playing with the hem of her shirt.

"You afraid to see me, Babygirl?" I ask her lowly and that gets her attention. Those beautiful blues find mine and for a moment, I feel everything all over again.

The undeniable lust, the tormented love, and finally, the loss. It all echoes in her doe eyes.

"Should I be?" she asks me, her cadence caressing. Her teeth sink into her bottom lip as she holds her breath waiting for my response. That lip I used to nibble as she moaned my name. Lips that used to kiss me and only me.

"You should leave." I push out the words, feeling a wash of cold run over my flesh. It comes back in waves, but the loss takes so much with it.

She swallows thickly with a nod and turns to leave without another word. Her thick hips sway and my gaze stays pinned to her until she disappears behind the double doors. She doesn't look back.

She never did.

"You fucked up." Derrick's deep voice carries over the beat of the music. His eyes stay glued to the television that displays over eight feet of the white and blue bars of an equalizer, changing with the rhythm.

It mocks me. The fact that everything in this place keeps moving, mocks me.

He takes a swig from his beer bottle, not bothering to look at me.

I have to close my eyes and breathe. Without her here, all that's left is anger.

I already know I fucked up. I take in a steadying breath as my teeth grind together.

The music keeps going. The women keep laughing.

My muscles twitch, consumed with a feeling of restlessness, the need to move, to do something.

"We both fucked up." Derrick's remark makes me open my eyes. Slowly and with a loathing for all of this, for everything I've built since she's been gone.

"Boss," Connor calls out, sliding a tumbler of whiskey over to me. I stare down at the glass, remembering everything. Watching it play out like a movie across the surface of the amber liquor.

Rowan calls out, "Boss," at the same time as someone else, but all I can picture is the night she left. The memory goes backward in time until I'm with her that morning, kissing her lips, feeling the dip of her waist. The voices around me lower in volume until I hear "Seth" instead.

There's never a minute. Never a quiet moment.

If there was, none of that shit would have happened.

I hear her tell me she loves me. I can practically feel her lips against the shell of my ear and the warmth that traveled down my shoulder that morning.

I didn't know I'd never feel that warmth again. I didn't know. But I should have.

It was all my fault.

With the single bellow of a roar torn from deep in my chest, I throw the glass in my hand recklessly at the flat-screen TV. The glass shatters, falling like rain, crashing into the liquor bottles lining the bar.

Connor and Rowan have to duck and cover their heads as I seethe, drawing in a breath and then another. I'd feel more remorse if she hadn't spoken to them, laughed with them. I'd feel guilty if she hadn't given her smiles to them so easily, when she didn't have a damn thing to give me.

I'm a bastard; I've always been a bastard.

"Get out," I say and my command ricochets in the large open space. Stunned faces stare back at me, the bar silent save for the occasional tinkling of glass shards. No one moves and that's their mistake too.

"Get the fuck out. We're closed." The low threat isn't hidden and a sea of women in short dresses suddenly start moving. No one looks at me for more than a split second as the patrons grab their shit and head for the door.

My crew stays where they are, their eyes on me. All but Derrick. He doesn't look at me. He takes a swig and stares at the broken TV as if it's still a visual for the non-existent music. Even as Connor and Roman ask me if I'm all right, I watch him staring blankly at the broken glass.

"If you want to help me," I begin as I finally look Roman in the eyes to answer him, feeling the rage subside but something else still lingers as I continue, "clean up this fucking mess."

The two men who are some of my best friends look at me with sympathy. I see it staring back at me in their eyes and it makes me grit my teeth. With the sound of my blood rushing through my ears, I grip the collar of Connor's shirt and bring the steadily spoken, low threat to his attention as I say, "Don't ever let her in here again."

CHAPTER 1

Thirteen months prior
Seth

M Y COCK IS STIFF IN THE MATTER OF A HALF second watching Laura do a feline stretch on my bed. The mattress protests with a groan until she settles down cross-legged and lays the book she's been studying in her lap. It looks heavy and uncomfortable, but I know she'll read it until she's tired, taking notes on that bright green pad of paper. She'll be tired enough that she stays, though. That's all I want.

"Why are you staring?" she asks and then taps the pen in her hand on the edge of the book. Once, twice, before looking up at me with a cocked brow. I was going to answer, but then she slips the end of the pen between her teeth.

She laughs at my groan and then reprimands me. "You're impossible."

"Maybe I just like seeing you on my bed," I offer her. Even with her tough-girl act, she smiles. "You're cute."

The way she sways slightly, reveling in the small statement does something to me. It took years to get to this point. Years of me fighting and struggling to feel stable.

Years of her by my side, carrying me along the way when I was too fucked in the head to see straight.

She glances down at her book and then back up at me. "Are you just going to keep watching me read?" Her tone is playful, a little taunting. It makes me that much harder.

I have to get out of here in thirty, meet the guys and tell them what's going down. I have time to enjoy her though.

I'll always make time for that.

"Lie down and spread your legs for me." I give her the command and wait for her reaction.

She bites down on her bottom lip, trying to contain her smile. Closing the hardback, she places it on the bedside table, scooting her glass to the side with the spine of the heavy anatomy textbook. "You like it, don't you?" she asks as she shimmies her way down the bed.

"Like what?" I ask her, feeling my cock twitch and not wasting another second to remove these jeans. I kick off the denim and pull my t-shirt over my head, noting how Laura's gaze drops down my chest, then to my boxer briefs the moment the shirt isn't in her way anymore.

I don't know if she does it on purpose or not, but the way she rocks her crossed legs from side to side on the bed, like she's impatient for me... fuck, I'm too hard.

"You like the dom thing?" she asks in a whisper and a blush sweeps up from her chest to her cheeks.

She asked me to try it out a few months ago. I tell her what to do. She listens.

"Fuck yeah I do."

I stare at her as I shove my briefs down. I love how she swallows when she sees my dick and her breathing gets deeper when I stroke myself.

"You already wet?" I ask her, a little cockier than I should be. With a little nod she hums an "uh-huh" in that seductive drawl she gets when I'm playing with her.

It takes a moment. It always does. Rocking in and out of her slowly, waiting for her to adjust, my skin is fire against hers as I rake my teeth up her slender neck. I can feel my warm breath in my face, followed by hers as I lazily kiss her. Taking my time, feeling her body writhe under mine. Her kiss is tender and sweet. Her nails dig into my shoulders, sending a slight pain that urges me to go in deeper. Once, twice, then her breath hitches, her doe eyes widen, and my name is a strangled moan in the air between us.

"There it is," I groan in her ear as she pushes her head back into the mattress. With each of my forearms pinned against her shoulders, I don't give her an inch of movement. When I pick up my pace, slamming myself deeper inside of her, she has nowhere to go.

"Take it, Babygirl," I grit between my teeth as I fuck her harder, faster, mercilessly. Feeling her warmth wrap around my cock, she's already screaming her pleasure in the crook of my neck.

I pound into her, feeling her climax and reeling in the way her cunt pulses around my cock. She's a damn good lover, urging me on and taking everything I have to give her.

With the steady pounding of the headboard against the wall, I pick up my pace, feeling my own release coming.

Not yet. I want her to cum again. I want to feel it all at least one more time.

I slow down, repressing my urge, going against everything I want.

And then I do it all over again.

My heart's racing and my blood ringing with adrenaline as I pick up my head to breathe when it's all over. She whimpers when I pull myself out of her, that sound I can't get enough of. Every sound she makes is like that. It's everything.

With her hair a messy halo and her eyes half lidded but still full of lust, she looks well fucked. She should always look just like this.

Checking the clock, I only have five minutes, but Laura will give me shit if I don't hold her for a minute. Her thighs shake when I clean her up.

My exhale is easy as I get back into bed, listening to it creak as Laura sidles up next to me.

It's quiet for a moment. I kiss her hair. She told me once it's what made her fall in love with me. When she was falling asleep, I kissed her hair. As if love is that easy.

"You going to get another this year?" she asks me as her fingertips run down the length of one of the bands across my right bicep. I have a sleeve of tattoos running from my wrist up to my shoulder, but around my bicep are three thin bands with untouched flesh between them. One for each year I won't ever forget. The first year, my mother died and the second, my father was murdered. The third year, I got revenge.

"Another band?" I question her, feeling a crease settle between my brow just as she nestles into me with a soft sigh. Her eyes never leave the tattoo.

"Yeah?" she asks.

It's been two years since my last tattoo. Because that's how long we've been together. Maybe she doesn't realize it's been that long. I sure as hell do though. I didn't get one last year. And I'm not planning on getting another.

It was all before this. These past two years have felt like… like after. There's no other way to describe it. She's here; I have my crew. There are no more demons left to fight. It's all just something I think of simply as after. "I think I might get something different," I answer her.

"You're running out of room," she humorously replies and looks up at me. Her pale blue eyes glimmer with affection. "Between the gears from your bike there might be a little space to put something."

A huff of a laugh leaves me and I settle back on the headboard, although the alarm clock tells me I'm already running late.

"Maybe I'll get something for you," I suggest and watch how she pulls back slightly to get a better look at my face. Her disbelief makes me smirk.

I grin as I whisper at the shell of her ear, "Don't be too scared."

"Not scared," she says, and pushes me away playfully as she answers. She still doesn't know if I'm serious or not and I like it that way.

Stretching my arms over my head, I roll out my shoulders and get out of bed. Grabbing my clothes, I get ready for tonight.

She looks surprised that I'm getting dressed. Shit, I didn't tell her. Sometimes she leaves when I'm gone, but damn do I want her to be here when I get back tonight.

Zipping up my pants and buttoning them, I explain, "I have to go meet up with the boys. You staying here to study?"

"Yeah, I really have to. If I do well, the advisor said I could apply to the nursing program and have a good shot."

"You will. You'll ace that shit."

She offers me a small smile but doesn't say anything. It's not like either of us were good at school. There was too much shit going on. Too much real shit that took up everything we had.

I get her insecurity, I understand it. But she's with me. No more of that. "You'll ace it, and then you'll move in with me," I tell her, as if saying it makes it an absolute.

Laura's eyes are silently warning me not to bring this

up and she bites the inside of her cheek. I don't push her; I don't have time to fight about this again.

Instead I pull my shirt down over my chest, lean over the bed, and give her a kiss. And then another with my hand spearing through her hair.

"You go to school. Be a fine-ass nurse. I can take care of us. Your schooling and all that."

My words are meant to reassure her, but the bright light that's always a constant in her eyes dims, as does her smile. She fights to keep it in place.

"I know you don't know how this is going to work. But I've got you. I've got us."

She's quiet and that doubt is still there. She wants a certain life—a quiet, honest living with white picket fences—a different one from this, but her place is with me. She knows it, I know it, everyone does. "I'll make sure you get everything you want. I promise," I tell her, and my voice is resolute.

"I love you," is all she responds. That, and a kiss that deepens then turns into more.

I'm going to be so fucking late.

CHAPTER 2

Laura

Every time I see this house, it hurts. The jingle of the keys and the sound of a car driving down the road behind me are all that I have to comfort me as I walk through the front door.

When I was a kid, I loved the slate floors of my grandma's house. I remember thinking the coffered ceilings were the kind of thing castles had. I remember rocking on the front porch swing and the thoughts I had of stealing Mr. Timms's roses from next door. His front yard was always prettier than Grandma's overgrown shrubs. She worked at the diner until the week she died. She didn't have time to smell the roses, let alone tend to them in her small front yard.

Whenever I'd pluck a few roses, Mr. Timms always knew it was me and Grandma would make me go over and apologize once he told her. Stubborn old man liked his garden.

That was then. Seen through the eyes of a child. I

know better now. It's a run-down house on a busy street in an old city. To add salt to the wound, the roses next door are grown over with weeds even though Mr. Timms still lives there. This street was destined for failure. I didn't know it back then, and I'm sure Grandma didn't see it when she bought the place after her husband of two years ran off with someone else and never looked back, abandoning her and her only son.

The train, the highways, the steel mill behind the development. It's all undesirable. My grandmother watched the neighborhood change as she aged. She hated what this town became when the steel mill went out of business decades ago and half the people here didn't have a job anymore.

I still remember the roses though. And I'll never take down that porch swing.

Shutting the door behind me, I take in what's left of her home. Half the furniture is gone since holding the last estate sale. I kept Grandma's chair though. I had it refurbished for her when the chemo stole her energy. I don't want to sit in the chair. I don't want to move it either.

I just want it to stay in the corner by the lamp where she read the newspaper and gossiped on the phone to Esme, another waitress from the diner.

Breathing out a tired sigh, I push off from the door and stare down at the bills in my hand. Grandma had plenty of them. And they keep coming.

I should sell this place, pay off the debts, and move in with Seth. At least that's what he says. But that's a little too much like moving on from the only person who was a constant in my life and putting all my faith in a man. A man who won't even tell me he loves me. Even if I love him, he scares me. All of this scares me.

The sound of the door creaking open startles me and I reward the newcomer with wide eyes and taking the Lord's name in vain.

It's only Cami.

"Shit," she says and cringes when she sees my hand over my chest. "Didn't mean to freak you out." She ducks her head a little with a grin as she shuts the door and says beneath her breath, "My bad."

"You could have knocked," I tell her and toss the stack of envelopes onto the side table at the entrance. It's butted up against the stairs that lead to the second floor. The hard maple side table has been there for years. When I was a kid, I thought about jumping off the balcony on the second floor and landing on the table. A neighborhood friend was chasing me when we were playing tag. I was a reckless and stupid girl. Hell, I'm still lacking in that department.

"Since when do I knock?" Cami walks right past me down the narrow hall and I follow her then stop when she gets to the kitchen. Leaning against the threshold and crossing my arms, I watch her open the fridge and take out a can of cola.

"You kinda look like hell," Cami comments with a wrinkled nose and then adds, "and you need to go grocery shopping."

"And to think… you're the bright light in my world," I say to mock my closest friend and her constant peppy tone.

She laughs as she cracks open the can, drinking soda at 9:00 in the morning. Her long blonde hair is a mess; it's obvious she hasn't brushed it yet, and she's still in her pajamas.

"You're looking rough yourself."

"Long night," she says cryptically and takes another sip, but she can't disguise the devilish smile she's hiding.

Her grin is infectious, and I join her at the small oak table in the kitchen.

"Shut up," I say then gasp as my eyes go wide. "Derrick?" I question her, feeling all those ooey gooey and excited emotions racing inside of me.

"Mm-hmm." She can't even speak as she nods her head. Beaming, her full lips are upturned as her cheeks turn red.

"Did you guys…?"

She shakes her head quickly and shoves the can of soda a few inches in front of her, looking at it and then me. "Not yet. I just don't want it to be a one-time thing, you know?" She talks quickly when she's nervous. Not even taking a breath, she continues. "He came over and we watched a movie. It was awful." She looks past me and shakes her head. "Like truly awful. I don't know why I let him pick." She breathes in for the first time, deep and easing the tension through her shoulders as she adds, "But it doesn't matter, because he pulled me in all close." She gets up and goes around the table. "Like this, you know," she tells me as she wraps her arm around my shoulders and makes me laugh.

"And then…" I draw out the last word, waiting for her to tell me the good stuff.

She shrugs, strutting back to her seat and taking a drink while she makes me wait.

"You're insufferable."

"And you love me."

I pull my lips into a grimace for half a second but then add, "I do love you."

"I love you too… and I loved it when he kissed me." She can't contain her giddiness as she practically dances in her seat. "Not even just once, but five times."

"Any makeout sessions?" I question and she nods as she replies, "Yup." The *P* pops as she says it. "Twice."

"So the yearlong crush is finally becoming something," I say then smile as I get up and search for coffee. I listen to Cami regale me with the details of last night, putting the grounds in the top and pushing the button to start the coffee maker.

"Slow and steady," Cami says, then downs the last of her soda and gets up to grab another one. "Not like you two," she adds.

The coffee machine hisses, and I couldn't agree more.

"Different strokes and all that," I half-heartedly reply. We did go too fast. It's hard to come back from all of that. We were both tumbling downhill, and there's no going slow when your life is free-falling. Better to fall fast together than apart.

"Any update on that matter?" she asks.

"Well since you're making out with his best friend…" I trail off and exhale heavily while I stir sugar into my coffee and the spoon clinks against the ceramic mug. "… you should know," I conclude before looking her in the eye.

Sitting back in her seat at the table, she asks me, "Seriously. You going to be okay?" Both of her hands are wrapped around the Coke can as she leans forward.

"You're so intense sometimes." I try to shake it off like Seth does, but Cami sees through me.

"Have you told him?" she asks.

I run my nail along one of the gouges in the wooden table as she talks. This table's been through a lot, but it's another thing I'll never get rid of. Grandma said it belonged to her mom. So, really, it's the only heirloom I've got. I've sat here and celebrated; cried and mourned. I sat here as I studied… even if I didn't do so well in school. The first kiss I ever had was in the kitchen threshold and shortly after that, Seth took me on this table.

Yeah, I'm never getting rid of this table.

"It's okay if you didn't."

I confess, "He knows."

"And?"

"And he was all… you know, as good as he could be about it." It hurts. Everything hurts, so I drink my coffee like it'll wash all these bad feelings down.

"It's a lot to go through at once."

"His solution is for me to move in with him, and he'll just take care of everything," I say as I toss my hand in the air and then stare down at my coffee through glossy eyes.

I won't tell her how he still didn't say it. He still didn't say that he loves me. It's so stupid, but with everything going on, it means so much to me that Cami's the only one in my life who will say it. She may be the only one to ever tell me those words again.

"Don't cry." Cami's voice is consoling. "You're going through a lot," she repeats.

"I'm not crying," I tell her a little too sternly and calm myself down, shaking out my hands. "I'm fine."

"You're not fine. And that's okay." Ever positive and nurturing. I love her, but she doesn't get it. We may both be in our early twenties, but she hasn't gone through an ounce of what I've seen in the last three years. Let alone my childhood.

"What am I going to do?" I ask her, not knowing myself.

"You think too much," she tells me after a long moment of silence.

"You don't think enough."

"That's not the first time you've said that," she jokes, and I let a puff of laughter leave me.

"First things first. You're going to study while I go through the bills. We have more than enough to pay the minimum on all of them…" She pauses as she hesitates but adds what I already know she's going to say, "I still think you should tell Seth. He would pay them off."

"And I'd be in debt to him and he'd have more of a reason for me to sell it all and give it all away."

She stares at me for a moment, not saying what's on her mind. Straightening in her seat, she drinks the rest of her second can of soda, making me even more jealous of how skinny she is. "You study, we pay the bills, and then we meet up with our men who are oh so bad for us and have a damn good time." She ends with a smile and the one I give her back is genuine.

"Yeah," I answer her, taking a sip of the much-needed coffee. "You're right. That's a good plan."

She gets up to toss her can in the recycling bin, but she stops where she is and turns to me with a serious expression. "I'm happy you told him."

I swallow the bitter coffee, not knowing what to say. Happy and that moment don't belong together.

CHAPTER 3

Seth

"WHAT'S UP WITH THIS GIRLY SHIT?" Derrick's voice bellows from behind me. He's not even through the front doors of this place and he's already being a prick.

I give it a moment, letting my eyes settle on his pale pink button-up paired with dark jeans. "You talking about that shirt you're wearing?"

It looks ridiculous. Derrick is jacked. He works out constantly and he was already built to be a big man.

He grunts a laugh and says, "The girl I'm seeing likes it. Fuck off." My chuckle is deep and short lived.

"Must really like this one," I comment. I've never known him to settle down or even remember the names of the different chicks he's with every week. Not until now. Times are changing, though. For all of us.

Standing in the middle of all this construction, of what will soon be my club, change is all I can think about.

"Girlfriend material?" I ask him.

"Something like that," he says, keeping his answer cryptic. Landing a hand on my shoulder, Derrick gives me a squeeze and adds, "Finally coming together, brother."

"That it is."

He squeezes again, commenting that the couch in the corner is too fucking girly for our club, as if he has any taste at all, and heads past me to the bar. It's not stocked yet, but the guys keep a stash on hand in the fridge. Drills are going, the TVs are being mounted, and the furniture is set in place now that the floors are down. The crew we hired is fast and on point.

Laura picked out the furniture, well most of it, including the sofa Derrick's not a fan of. It'll all come together. She shares my vision, and the guys will get on board.

Cracking open a bottle and tossing the cap into the bin with a clink, Derrick's voice echoes as he asks, "Where are the fights going to be?"

Selling guns is how we got this far, old business that was set in stone when we took over, but the fighting and betting? That's a steady flow of cash I didn't know was possible. A bar to push the dirty money through is the cherry on top.

"It's called underground for a reason," I answer him and steal his beer before he takes his first swig.

"Fucker," he comments when I tell him thanks.

"Grab yours and follow me," I tell him just as Connor

comes in. He's got his sleeve rolled up and I can see the shamrock tat on the inside of his forearm. He's Irish through and through. He even gave me shit about having Mexican beer in the bar. *What Irish pub carries Dos Equis?* Ours does, because it's damn good beer.

I've got five guys in my crew. We started this shit together; we'll always be together. Growing up in this town, we saw how things were run. It took one too many blows but now it's ours. Simple as that. Connor's got a scar on the left side of his jaw to prove it. He's the shortest of us, the leanest too, but he's the one I'd pick in a knife fight. Ten out of ten times. The Irish in him, that crazy bastard side, gives him the edge he needs.

Together, the five of us own this town. And this bar is going to be the crowning jewel of our empire.

Connor takes a look around and I watch him, waiting for his reaction. He moves the pack of beer in his right hand to his left and then back again.

"What do you think?" I ask.

"Legit cash flow in the bar, fight club downstairs. It's perfect."

"You like that girly-ass sofa? A fucking sofa in a bar?" Derrick says and regards Connor, who looks in his eyes and then at his shirt.

"What the hell are you wearing?" Connor asks.

"Screw both of you," Derrick says and shoves his beer into Connor's chest then starts unbuttoning his shirt. He tosses it on the back of a sleek steel barstool, its seat lined with cobalt velvet.

Wearing just his white t-shirt on top, he leaves the button-up where it is and snags back his beer.

"Don't feel peer pressured now," I quip and make my way to the back left of the large open space, past the bathrooms that are being renovated and I head down a narrow hall. The sound of construction dims until it's nonexistent as we hustle down the steel stairs. It's nothing but luxury on the first floor, or at least it will be, but down here, it's raw and primitive.

With a flick of the switch, the lights come on; thin rails of white light form stripes along the ceiling. They go from wall to wall so nothing will be missed. Spotlights will be installed next. Everything's on schedule.

"Ring in the center. Stage at the back for security to watch over everything. We'll be here at the head, calling the shots." I can see it all play out. It's only cement floors and drywall with spackle at the moment, but I can already hear the bell going off, the cheering, the crunch of bone.

"Vale Tudo," Connor says as he makes his way around the back of the basement. It's nearly a two-hundred-foot square.

"What the hell does that mean?" Derrick asks; he has to speak up as Connor's halfway down the room and Derrick's coming up beside me. He's my right-hand man. My best friend. I wouldn't be here without him. He wouldn't be here either. And we both know it.

"Anything goes… It's Portuguese fighting."

My answer comes without a second thought, "Oh, fuck that."

"Eye gouging and nut kicking... No, sir," Derrick comments.

Connor laughs and bellows from the back of the room, "Pussies."

"Seriously, though," Derrick says and holds up his beer as if he's toasting, "it's going to be killer." Derrick looks around even though I hadn't broken eye contact with him and I take him in. It's been a long damn time since he's been like this. Carefree and relaxed.

"Things are finally looking up," he comments as he looks around the room and Connor makes his way to us.

"You need a beer," he tells me, taking out a beer for me and then cracking one open for himself. It fizzes and he curses as he sucks the head from the top of the beer to keep it from spilling.

Derrick laughs at him and I take a moment to open mine carefully so I don't suffer the same fate.

"This is it, boys. We have the legit business from the bar, but this gets us in deeper, so we know what's going on and we have the cash to stay in the thick of it."

"That it is," Derrick says and then asks me, "Speaking of the thick of it. You hear from Wright?"

"That's why I wanted you two here, away from the construction crew upstairs."

"Figured as much," Connor comments.

My shoulders feel tighter as I lift the beer to my

mouth but stop short of taking a sip. "He said Mathews is storing everything at the docks."

"All of it's there?" Derrick asks just beneath his breath.

"All but the cash. That he keeps in a safe in his house."

"We don't need to go for the cash, right?" Connor clarifies.

"Right. Just his drugs. He's growing too quickly, taking up too much territory and getting too close for comfort."

"Time for him to take a hit," Derrick says.

"And then another," I add.

"Where in the docks?" Connor questions.

"Roman staked it out last night. He knows right where it is. He said two men stayed there all night. A pair of dogs too."

"Fuck, not dogs," Derrick groans and grimaces. He got his leg torn up pretty good by a dog a few years back.

"It'll be taken care of. Don't worry," I reassure him. "In and out. We grab the haul and go."

"You think he'll know it was us?"

"Nah, we're throwing it out. We don't need his shit supply. It's laced up and cut so much it's hardly worth a dime. He's going to be looking for someone selling."

"Good," Connor says.

"When are we going?"

I look at Derrick to answer his question. "Tonight.

Let the girls come here and we'll have Roman keep an eye on them. We'll go out and take care of it. Come back when we're done and no one will be the wiser."

All three of us grew up in this life. All three of our fathers died going against the men who took over. Men who didn't belong here and didn't give a damn about the people who live here. It was only a matter of time before we took this place back.

Revenge was sweet, but cleaning out this place the last two years has been hard as hell. People like Mathews need to stay back and this is how that happens. They inch closer, we steal their shit, wreck their warehouses, kill their men. We make it unprofitable and violent. We do whatever we have to in order to never go back to what used to be.

"No one owns Tremont but us," Derrick declares.

"Damn right," I tell him and clink my beer with his.

Connor lifts his beer and Derrick and I follow suit as he starts our toast. "Here's to the money, the dirty and the clean."

Derrick goes next. "Here's to the women, the ones who please us and the ones who make us scream."

I finish it out. "And here's to chaos, may we make that bitch our queen."

CHAPTER 4

Laura

"THREE HUNDRED IS LEFT OVER," CAMI TELLS me and points to the spreadsheet on her computer. Her chipped pink nails are a sign of the stress I know she's feeling right now. She put it all together, accounting for every cent of the money coming and going.

With my shoulders relaxed, I play off every bit of anxiousness that's been pulling me down, hoping to give her a little lift up. She doesn't need to carry my burdens. Damn do I love her for doing it though.

"So that's three hundred for the next two weeks to live off of after all the bills. That seems good, right?"

"After gas and food… that's tight, but it's workable," she confirms.

"And you're sure they're okay with just fifty a month?" I ask her again and then I want to kick my ass for second-guessing her and bringing in "bad mojo," as she'd call it.

"The hospitals?" she questions. Nodding, she makes her voice seem more chipper than it has been. "Yeah, they'll settle for what you can afford. Fifty a month for these bills is... appropriate. Insurance doesn't cover it. Eight bills total, so four hundred a month to cover someone else's medical bills. That's what you can afford... Barely."

"At least the new bar is coming." I'm trying to be optimistic as I sit back at the kitchen table. I stare through the threshold to the large bay window at the front of the living room. It needs new trim and the whole house could use a fresh coat of paint. Everywhere I look I see dollar signs and evidence that times are changing.

"Right. When the new bar comes, you'll make more money bartending. For now, you have the Clubhouse... and... and Seth... if you ask him."

I move my gaze back to Cami. "I don't want to ask him."

"He's—"

"Not yet," I say to cut her off. "I just... just give me time to figure everything out," I plead with her to understand. I don't want to be indebted to Seth more than I already am. Even if I love him, I still need a sense of independence. Especially now.

I have nothing but this little piece of independence. As small and shitty as it is, it's mine still. If it's gone, all I am is Seth's girl. If I don't pass this test, I'll never be anything but his girl. His burden too.

I don't ever want to be anyone's burden. Not like my father was. I will always love him and I hate to think ill of the dead, but it is what it is. He was a burden to my grandma. Hell, he was a burden to me. I won't be that. I won't allow it.

"I get it," Cami says. Breathing in, she taps her empty can on the table at the same time as I see a bright red shirt on my porch.

"What the fuck?" I can feel confusion line my face and then recognition when what's happening dawns. My heart races. "Who the hell is that?" I whisper the question and Cami turns to look out of the window too.

I see the guy's profile; I don't recognize him or his shaggy hair. And then I see my bike. In his hands.

"He's stealing my bike!" I jump out of my chair so fast it falls onto the floor, clattering as I rush past Cami and make my way to the door.

Bat, bat, bat. It's a mental reminder I scream in my head with every step. It isn't the first time in this neighborhood I've needed an edge on my side.

I keep a baseball bat between two umbrellas in the entry stand. Hating the feel of it in my hands, but damn grateful to have it, I snatch it and then unlock the door. Feeling a wave of disgust and anger rush through me, I watch the guy walk out into the middle of the street, both of his hands on MY bike and surrounded by a man on each side of him.

"Hey!" I scream out in the street, hearing my front door slam open and then shut behind me. "Hey fuckers!" I yell louder, my footsteps pounding down the uneven stone steps as I hustle my ass toward them in the middle of the street. The bat is in my hand, swaying heavily, but my grip is white knuckled on it.

It doesn't escape me that if it was just one of them, he could get on the bike and take off, but as it is, all three guys turn around and face me.

One of the assholes has a broad and gorgeous smile on his baby face. Freshly shaven or incapable of growing hair on his chin, I don't know. And I don't care. The asshole is smiling at me. That's when I notice his eyes are red. So are the guy's next to him. With blond hair down to his shoulders, the second guy looks like he doesn't give a shit about anything. He's just here for the ride.

The one holding the bike looks me up and down like, "What are you going to do about it?" with the same bloodshot eyes.

They're young. Young and dumb. I may be around their age, but age is a number, while youth is inexperience. The shit we've gone through—Seth, me, the crew—it's enough to age someone decades. We've been through more than some people go through their entire lives. These guys in front of me? I can see in their eyes that they haven't experienced the turmoil life is.

Three assholes out for a walk, high as fucking kites and taking what they want along the way as a joke.

My life isn't a joke. They don't get to take from me. No one gets to take from me.

The adrenaline causes the blood to course too fast through my veins. I can barely breathe, barely keep from shaking I'm so furious.

"Laura!" Cami's yelling my name from the porch, but I don't turn around. I'm not taking my eyes off these bastards.

"That's my bike." I grit out the words, my chest heaving.

"Looks like it's his now," the first guy says, and the others laugh. They laugh at me. "Possession is nine-tenths of the law," one of the others says. Even glancing down at the bat in my hand, the bat that sways slightly and brushes against my leg, they continue to laugh.

Taking one deep inhale full of rage and disbelief, I whip the bat above my head and crash it down onto the bike. I don't think twice. I just do it.

It's all the hurt and bitterness inside. I let it out. There are times to contain and times to explode. I'm hoping this is one of the latter, because I do it again. Screaming incoherently all the while.

I land the bat down with tired, aching muscles that somehow find explosive energy in the single act. The wooden bat is raised and swung.

Crashing down upon the bike my dad taught me to ride on before he died.

Smack! The wood hits the asphalt and the shock from the impact travels up my arms.

I used to ride it to his grave after the car accident. The memory brings a prick to the back of my eyes. Maybe this is what I get for thinking ill of him. Instant karma. The universe decided I wasn't allowed to have the bike anymore.

I lift the bat again, hearing the men back away. Calling me crazy. With both hands on the bat, I swing with everything I have, hitting the gears, smashing the handlebars again and again.

All I can hear is my frantic breathing and Cami telling me to calm down, saying that I'm all right.

With hot tears streaming down my face, I look up to see the three men looking more awake, more sober than they were when they stole from me.

"Now it's no one's fucking bike," I spit at them, tossing the busted bat at their feet then moving to walk away.

"Get out of here!" Cami screams at them. Her hand on my shoulder is soothing in some ways. I don't think I can speak right now.

"Are you deaf?" Cami urges them on when they hesitate, staring at me like I'm a sight to behold. Sometimes when you take from people, you take more than just a dumb bike.

They don't care. Or at least they didn't.

I wonder if they'll laugh and grab something off of another person's porch again.

The tears keep coming, but I don't brush them away; I won't give them that satisfaction of watching me clean myself up. I'm fine like this. I'm just fine.

I watch them leave, picking up their pace as they get closer to the street corner. Occasionally, they turn around to see if I'm still here. And I am. Standing right where I was when they left and waiting for them to disappear.

I don't even realize Cami's cleaning up my bike until I hear the clink of the broken gears against the metal trash can she dragged into the middle of the street. I'm grateful that this time of day isn't busy. Because heaven forbid a car come down this road now and beep at me or tell me to get out of the way. I can still feel the thrum of anger.

It's a good thing I put that baseball bat down. I don't like it. I just want it to go away. I don't like this side of me.

"I lost it," I say then finally swallow the sharp pains in my throat and wipe under my eyes. Falling to my knees I help pick up the mess, the tiny bits of metal and the bent wheel, the splinters of wood. All the small pieces go in the trash can.

There are also some pieces under my knees. They dug into my skin. I guess with the adrenaline, I didn't even feel it.

"Those guys were assholes," is all Cami says. But she knows, just like I know, that I lost it.

"And to think, I thought my anger issues were dealt with," I joke and that makes her laugh although the sound is choked.

She hugs me tight, both of us still on our knees in the middle of the street. "You okay?" she whispers.

Although I nod and pull away, hurrying to clean up, I'm not okay. I haven't been okay for a while now.

I feel hot and my head is light when I finally stand up and drag the bent, broken bike to the curb. Sniffling, I wipe the rest of the tears from my heated face.

I barely look over my shoulder when I hear a car pull

up. "Fuck," I murmur and roll my eyes when I see who it is.

"What the hell is going on?" I can hear Seth freaking out before his door even shuts. The slam seems like an overreaction as it echoes down the street.

My heart's all sort of wonky. Hurting and flipping and full of distress. *So much for not being a burden.*

"What the hell happened? You okay?" He's staring between the bike and me. My legs that aren't scratched, my elbows that aren't bruised. He's trying to figure it out, I know he is, but right now I can't speak. How the hell did my bike get so damaged when I'm seemingly fine, although I'm sure it's obvious I've been crying?

"Babygirl," he says and his voice is consoling as he cups my chin and then brushes away the remaining tears.

"I'm fine," I tell him and then I have to clear my throat. My voice is so raw. "I didn't fall. I…"

"She took a bat to it," Cami finishes for me. She takes a seat on the stone steps to the porch, brushing her hands off on her pajamas. "Some guys tried to steal it and your girl lost it."

"What guys?" Seth's voice turns stone cold.

"Three assholes. Never seen them before." Cami does all the talking, even though she pauses to look at me. I can't look her in the eyes as my gaze drops.

"You fuck them up?" Seth asks. His voice is even, low but even. He just wants to know; he's not judging me. God, do I love this man. I shake my head in his hand and then move from his grasp. I don't deserve him.

39

Taking a deep inhale, I calm myself.

"I just lost it," I explain to him.

"So you wrecked your bike?"

"Better the bike than them, right?" I try to make it sound like a joke. He doesn't think it's funny though. There goes my gaze, back to the weeds in the cracks of the sidewalk.

"I mean, you should have seen it," Cami butts in before Seth can reply. I feel embarrassed, guilty, remorseful. My stomach churns and I feel sick. "I can guarantee you they think she's crazy."

"You should have called me—"

I cut Seth off. "They aren't going to steal from me again." Finally looking him in the eyes, I tell him, "They aren't coming back here and taking things off porches again."

In my periphery, I can see Cami nodding, although her expression is solemn.

"I handled it," I say with finality.

Seth shifts his weight, staring down at me. He feels very much like the judge, jury, and executioner right now. As if that's what I need.

"What would you do if someone stole your pen?" he asks me as Connor's car pulls up behind Seth's. I barely keep from rolling my eyes, knowing Seth must've called or messaged and told him to come. All because I'm a little messed up right now.

"My pen?" I say, trying to remember what the question even was.

"Like next time, say someone steals your pen. What are you going to do?"

I imagine someone at the Club doing that. Not like they took it accidentally after signing their check. But deliberately taking from me... at the Club? No one would be that stupid.

"There won't be a next time," I say and my voice holds an edge to it. Seth closes the distance between us with a few easy steps. Placing a hand on each of my forearms, he squeezes, consoling and relaxing.

Pulling me in closer to him, he gentles his voice. "Just humor me. Say someone steals your pen, what are you going to do?"

"Take it back." He nods at my response but then I add, "And then stab the hand they took it with. I'd keep stabbing that hand with the same pen until there was nothing left of the pen anymore."

Seth's eyes widen comically, but the Cheshire cat smile grows on his face even more. "You're psycho, Babygirl."

"I'm joking. Ish." The "ish" makes Cami laugh. The tension in the air seems to dissipate.

Seth's smirk widens to a grin and I give him a small smile in return.

"Come here," he says and holds me against his chest, wrapping his arms around me. I didn't even realize how cold it was outside today until I feel how warm he is.

"Next time, call me," he whispers into my hair. "Please."

"There won't be a next time," I answer into his chest, breathing in his scent. The essence is fresh but masculine. And if I breathe in deeper, I can smell a hint of the cologne I got him for Christmas. I heard smell is the scent most likely to hold memories. With everything that's happened while I've been at Seth's side, you'd think they'd all be bad. Like the smell of him would bring me nothing but pain. It's the opposite though. I feel safe, I feel cherished. I never want to forget the smell of him. I wish I could bottle it up and put it in an aromatherapy roller ball or something.

"You're adorable but fucking psycho, you know that?"

I pull away at his comment. "What was I supposed to do? Let them steal my bike?"

Any worry he had when he arrived has turned to a smile. "I would have gotten it back for you and made sure they knew never to do that shit again."

"Well you weren't here, so I did it for you." I stand on my tiptoes for a quick second to offer him a peck. Although the kiss is more for me than him, I think. "You're welcome," I add with a little more sass than I should have right now.

"Mmm." His groan is more than a turn-on and he grabs my ass before I can turn around and leave him like I planned on doing. Pinning me to him, he tells me, "I'm not done with you yet."

The spike of heat and want is immediate. A feeling of calm washes over me. I could stare into his soft blue eyes forever. Well, I can try. But when he leans down for another kiss, I close my own and let him press his lips to mine. He nips the bottom one and when I smile, he takes that as his cue to deepen the kiss. The embrace is heated and brings a singe of desire that overwhelms every other feeling.

"My little hotheaded psycho," he murmurs when he breaks the kiss, his lips still close to mine.

"Stop," I say and jokingly push him away, but both of us are smiling. "I'm not psycho," I tell him and I finally roll my eyes, although of course it's in response to my own statement. I really lost my shit. Over a bike. It's just a bike.

"Yeah, you are. I fucking love it, though."

There's that word. *Love.* He didn't say he loves me. Not quite, but it feels like he did.

"You two need a room?" I hear Connor's question laced with heavy sarcasm before I hear his footsteps stopping just behind Seth.

"If I wind up dead in a gutter, she did it," Seth tells Connor, not answering his question.

"Oh, fuck off," I tell him playfully as Seth laughs at my reaction. He's good at soothing me, teasing me, working me up. He's good at *me*. That's the best way I can put it. Turning to look over my shoulder as I make my way up the steps, I tell Seth as they follow me into the house, "I'm going to leave long before I reach my breaking point with you."

CHAPTER 5

Seth

"YOU WANT TO TALK ABOUT IT?" I ASK HER, watching her strip out of her clothes to get into the shower. She's still in her old room in her grandma's house, even though the master's been cleared out.

I get it, I do. I've stayed plenty of nights here and I know this is her place. It's her safe spot. I get it.

This room is just small. She's got a twin-size bed and barely any room in here with her bulky dresser. She has to have the damn dresser because there are no closets in this old house.

She wrinkles her nose at me, as if I'm pushing her too far. She's the one always asking me to talk, though.

"Is that a no, you don't want to talk?"

"No." The way she eyes me before answering puts a smug look on my face. She's not psycho, she's defensive and scared. After everything that happened these last few years, she should be.

"All right then," I tell her and lean back in her bed,

taking up the whole damn thing as I stretch out my shoulders and stare at her ceiling fan. "What'd they look like?" I question her even though she's not going to tell me. She doesn't have to say a word though, because I told Connor to get the descriptions from Cami. I'll figure it out and make sure they don't ever make my girl feel like that again. She doesn't have to know. She just needs to be safe.

"I don't remember," she answers half-heartedly, shrugging her shoulders as she steps into the stream of the shower. With the bathroom door open, I've got a great view from where I'm lying.

I think about talking louder over the running water, of pressing her again on whether or not she's going to sell this place. It's not the right time though. It's never the right time with her.

The house is in a rough part of town, every piece of it. From the staircase that creaks, to the trim that's dented and stained, it's all worn down, but the old home is sentimental. If she wants to keep it, we can. Shit, I'll even fix it up. I want her with me though. In my house that she helped me build, that *she* furnished. I got that damn house for her.

Isn't that what compromise is?

I'm debating about approaching the subject, when I turn over and see her family photo on the dresser. Her dad, her grandma, and her at some park when she was just a kid. I get that this house is all she's got left of them. I swear I do. I just don't like it.

Now's not the time, but I don't know when it will be time though. Shit.

Pinching the bridge of my nose, I listen to the water splashing and talk over it, raising my voice to make sure Laura can hear me.

"You really shouldn't pick fights." I don't tell her it scares me. I don't tell anyone that anything scares me.

"You can stop reprimanding me," she calls out in a singsong voice after opening the sliding glass door to make sure I hear her response. The shower door closes and then opens again for her to add, "And I didn't pick the fight, I finished it."

Her smart-ass mouth brings a warmth to my chest as I chuckle and run a hand down my face. She shouldn't have to finish any fights. That's the problem.

It's my fault for letting her stay here.

Letting her. She hates that word.

Now there's a real fight to pick. Not tonight though. Not with everything going down.

The creak of the faucet precedes the sound of the water stopping, the shower door sliding open and the pitter-patter of her bare feet in the bathroom.

I watch her dry herself off, then wrap her hair up in the towel. All the while, I eye her curves. She takes her time rubbing lotion into her legs and I'm pretty sure she's prolonging touching herself just to tease me.

She dries her hair and lets the towel drop to the floor in a puddle at her feet. With one hand on either side of the threshold, she stands there butt naked, looking utterly fuckable. And then she speaks.

"You don't fuck with crazy."

Grabbing my hard cock through my jeans I tell her, "Speak for yourself."

She gives me a ridiculously gorgeous smile that's infectious and tells me I'm awful before making her way to the bed.

"Come here." I give her the command even though she was already coming to me.

She crawls up my body, slow and deliberate, but keeps her hair to the side since it's still damp.

"You really are impossible," she tells me and she could be saying I'm her Prince Charming with the look she's got in her eyes. I love the way she looks at me. No one's ever looked at me like that before. No one other than her.

"I don't think you've got much room to talk," I respond, wanting to bring up the situation again if for no other reason than to get her fine ass to move in with me and be safe.

"When I said that, I meant no one wants to mess with a crazy person," she explains. "That's what my dad used to tell me. You never know what someone crazy is going to do. They could bite your nose off if you push them, you know? They're crazy. So if you react like that, like you've lost your mind, no one's going to want to mess with you. It's not worth losing your nose over."

I have a hard time keeping a straight face; she's serious as all hell right now. "So you were *acting* like you're crazy? You were in full control the whole damn time?" I question her, letting my tone prove that I think what she's saying is bullshit.

Pursing her lips she thinks for a moment, looking past me. Instead of answering me, she says, "I didn't pick the fight." The humor and confidence are gone.

"I know you didn't," I tell her with sincerity. Spearing my hand through her hair, I bring my lips to hers and kiss her. I nudge my nose against hers and whisper, "You did what you had to do."

"Exactly." Both of her hands wrap around mine when she speaks. And I kiss her again, but she pulls away.

"I have to get ready," is the excuse she gives me. Her ass sways as she walks, tempting me even though she doesn't seem interested.

"You wanna?" I ask her, and when she turns to look at me with a hint of confusion, I thrust my hips in her direction.

She only laughs before telling me no and saying I'm a shitty Romeo.

"What if I kiss you here?" Getting on my knees at the edge of the bed so I can tower over her as she stands at the end of it, I suck her neck. I feel her thighs hit the edge of the bed and hear her moan before I plant a single kiss there and pull back.

"You're hot," she tells me with a moan and smiles. "But I don't want to be late, and you're not getting laid right now. You should come up with something better while I'm getting dressed."

Damn it. I watch her walk away.

"You know all my lines already," I call out to her as she closes the bathroom door, leaving me with blue balls

48

in her too-small bed. Even being shut down I'm smiling, because she's all right and she's happy.

We're all right. Everything is going to be all right.

Not even five seconds pass before the bathroom door opens again. I only raise up my head, to look at her.

She clucks her tongue and puts both hands on the door again. Her small breasts have a bit of weight to them and they sway when she sways.

"Sometimes I do feel crazy," she tells me and I see the hurt there, plain as day in her eyes as they gloss over.

"You're not crazy," I say. I'm quick to sit up but before I can get off the bed, she's already walking to me. I wait there on the edge, the bed bowed in the center from my weight.

She stops before she can walk between my knees. When she's hurt, all I want to do is love her. Lay her down and fuck her until the sad eyes are only in my memory.

Crossing her arms, her breasts are pushed up. She is not helping my situation at all. "Tell me what you need, Babygirl," I speak softly and caress her, placing a hand on each of her elbows. I know what she needs.

She finally decides on her next words. "I love you, and you need to make this up to me."

"Get on the bed," I tell her, standing up so she can take my place.

"That's not—"

"Get your ass on that bed." I'm firmer this time and she can't hide the smile. She gets on the bed on all fours before rolling onto her back and lying down for me.

"Knees bent, legs spread," I tell her, and the grin widens even with her teeth sinking into that bottom lip.

I make my way between her legs; she has to move her heels out further so my shoulders fit between her knees.

I start with a single kiss on the inside of her knee. "Let me show you how much I worship this…" I say then pause to plant another kiss, further up her thigh.

She's already breathing heavy, already wriggling on the bed ever so slightly.

I smack her clit with the back of my hand. Her top half jolts up, her eyes go wide and her mouth drops open. "Keep still," I tell her and push her chest back down. She obeys.

She says she wants a dom; I'll give it to her.

"Like I was saying," I say and plant another kiss on the inside of the opposite knee. "Let me show you how much I worship…" I keep my warm breath close to her skin as I speak and watch the goosebumps slide up her body, following my path of open-mouth kisses.

"… This perfectly sane…" I can't even keep a straight face while I talk, so I smile against her skin. The warmth of her feminine laugh and the way she covers her face fuel me to continue.

Another kiss. "Never unreasonable…" I say and shake my head between her thighs, letting my nose graze just above her clit.

"Completely stable…" I continue then suck on her clit, which cuts off her laughter instantly.

Her legs close tighter around me, and I push them back open, reminding her to be still.

"Beautiful," I add and plant another kiss. "Smart," I say and lick her from her entrance to her hard nub. "Woman," I say then breathe against her clit while her hands find my hair. Pulling on what little she can grab, I don't stop sucking and licking until she's trembling under me.

Then I take her like I have so many times. On this too-small bed, in this broken-down house, filled with so many memories just like this. Lying next to her when it's all over, I think again about how I get it, even if she thinks I don't. I get why she wants to stay.

"You're not coming in?" Laura questions me when I stop the car at the front of the Clubhouse. I haven't even put it in park yet, but she knows the drill. She turns off the radio and looks at the Club and then back at me. The Club is an old bar Connor's dad used to own. He had bikes and he liked to think of him and his friends as a motorcycle club. Connor inherited it when they were gunned down. This place is everything that represents how we got here. We inherited what was ours to have and the life that comes with it.

"We just have to run and pick something up," I lie.

Laura clucks her tongue after unbuckling her seat belt. Narrowing her beautiful eyes, she tells me, "You picked me up so I wouldn't drive here. So I couldn't leave while you were out doing something stupid."

"Beautiful and smart," I say then tilt my head to the side and give her a charming smile. "How'd I get so lucky?"

"What are you doing, Seth?" she asks and her tone is serious.

"Just something stupid. I'll be quick, I promise. You won't even get your second drink down before I'm back." I give her a quick kiss that she doesn't return, and her expression is the same as it was when I lean back.

She settles into her seat, her clutch in her lap and she looks at me. Really looks at me. "I wish you wouldn't do dumb shit."

I can't return her gaze when I lie to her. I'm staring at my thumb tapping restlessly on the steering wheel instead as I say, "I'm working on it."

I'm getting in deeper. That's the way this works. There isn't an out. One day she'll see that. She just needs time to adjust.

The leather protests as she leans over the console and plants a kiss on my jaw. "Don't get yourself hurt," she tells me and then gets out of the car without sparing me another glance.

I promise her I won't and watch her go. She looks back and gives me the smallest of smiles. I know it's more for me than it is her. Or at least that's how it feels in this moment.

I keep the radio off as I drive away after watching her walk in. Roman was at the door, so he's got her taken care of. The twenty-minute drive is quiet on the way to the warehouse. Nothing but black night and cool spring air blowing from the open windows.

Quiet is good for moments like this. Preparing for the "dumb shit," as she calls it. I go over the plan with every turn I take until I'm parked beside two unmarked vans behind Linel Centers.

"Already got the plates," Derrick tells me when I get out. There's nothing back here in the mountains but woods. Crickets chirp in the distance as I open up the double doors to see the back of the van is empty. It's colder than it was when I left Laura. Seems fitting.

"Other one is empty too," Derrick tells me and then Connor appears, the keys to the other van clattering in his hand. "We're all set, Boss."

"What about the fireworks?" I ask them and Connor tells me those are all set too.

"All right, let's do this." I give the command as I shut the doors, but Derrick grabs my arm. "What about the dogs?"

Half of me wants to mess with him, tease him about being scared of some dogs, but tonight is all business. "Tranqs are in the glove box of my car. Grab 'em."

Derrick pats my shoulder and I can see the instant relief on his face. While he's off getting the tranquilizer guns, I tell Connor to take that van and I'll ride with Derrick.

This isn't the first time we've done this shit. Won't be the last. Roman and Liam are at the Club, but they're on call and they know it. Sometimes in our line of business, the more, the better. But late at night, in the dark with a surprise like this, the fewer, the better. We only need three.

I probably could have done it with just two, but someone needs to be driving and someone else on the walkie while we're moving. So three it is. Besides, I don't know how much shit Mathews has in his stores.

Reaching in my jacket pockets, I hand Connor one of the two walkie-talkies. "Let's do this."

The gravel crunches under my boots as I round the back of the van and I look up to the moon. Not a star is in sight, just vacant dusk and a sliver of light. Every five minutes I swear the night sky is getting darker.

"You drive," I tell Derrick and hear Connor close his door. He starts his van before Derrick can move. The empty van sways as Derrick swings himself into his seat.

"You good? Got your mask?" I speak into the walkie and pull my mask from the glove box. It's a simple ski mask. I'm sure there are cameras, so we're taking every precaution. I don't have to wait long for a response.

"All good, Boss."

The van revs to life and four streams of white brighten the dirt road ahead of us.

With the walkie's talk button pressed down, I speak to both of them, going over the plan one more time.

"As soon as we're lined up at the docking site, Connor will set off the first round of rockets a block down. They're all set, right, Connor?"

"Got 'em in place. And they're the best ones too. They're low and sound like gunshots."

I wait for the click and continue. "There are only two men on-site and they stay out of the storage unit. I bet Mathews is too scared one of his men will steal from him, so he keeps it light. We get their attention with the fireworks. They run toward the noise or to their cars, I don't give a shit where, so long as they're far enough back and going after something that isn't there. We back the truck up, over the fence and right into door of the storage building at the dock. In and out, no talking. Not a damn word unless someone's going to die. Got it?"

"Got it," they both answer without stress, with nothing but seriousness.

"We'll take this shit back here, dump it, change the plates, and head back to the Club like nothing happened."

"It's a plan," Derrick comments as we round the corner, getting us out of here and where we need to go.

It's silent while we drive. Just like the drive down here. All the while, I let the adrenaline flow. It courses through me, urging me to get it done as quick as we can without missing a beat. I glance at Derrick, whose hard expression mirrors what I feel. It's why this crew works; we all need the same, want the same. I focus on the plan and why we need Mathews to back the hell up. This will hurt him and it'll make him think twice about inching closer to Tremont.

Time goes by too fast, but not fast enough just the same.

I can already smell the water. There's a saltiness to the air with the windows down. We have five minutes until we're there. If that.

Five minutes of calm although it feels anything but. My muscles are tense and my throat tight. This spike in my veins is a different kind of high. My second favorite. The only thing that tops this is when I'm under Laura. Or on top of her, for that matter.

This right here, I fucking love the intensity. The need to fight severely, quickly. The desire to protect what's ours… It will never grow old. It's everything. Laura should know that. She just needs time.

When Derrick sees me putting on my gloves, he does the same. One block to go, and the small bait store on the corner comes into view. The fixture is an old shed and shut down for the night. Everything down here is closed. There shouldn't be any witnesses. Other than the two men working for Mathews.

"Masks on," I tell them and put on my own. It's hot with it in place, but a necessity. Just like the gloves. The mask is cheap, but my gloves are thin leather and expensive as shit. I can't have gloves slipping off or hindering my movements when I'm in the heat of it all.

Thump, my heart pounds in my chest, fighting against my rib cage as we come around the corner. There are three white storage sheds made of steel. Each surrounded by chain-link fences ten feet high. They look about twenty feet apart from each other. One has two dogs inside the perimeter, with a doghouse in the far corner. That's it.

There are two men on that property. At least there should be, but I don't see either of them yet.

"Here," I speak into the walkie and watch as Connor's van comes to a stop in the rearview. We're in a good position to keep a lookout and not be seen. Turning off the vans, we wait.

This is the worst part. The waiting. Not being able to move.

We need eyes on the men doing patrols. I wait a minute and then another, feeling the ring in my blood, the need to be fast and not sit and wait. It could be a setup. Wright could be two-timing us. The glance from Derrick tells me he's on edge just like I am.

We can't wait. When you're still, that's when your enemies catch up to you.

"Now." The second I say the word, I catch sight of a man coming around the corner of the dock. Smoke billows from his blunt as he rounds the building from inside the fence.

Crack, crack, crack!

The rockets go off somewhere unseen, but they hit the building farthest away from the one we're after.

The man screams what sounds like a name, dropping his smoke and grabbing the gun at his waist. He races to the gate of the fence furthest from us. His back is to us; he doesn't have a clue we're here.

So far, it's all going according to plan, but anything can go wrong.

Wait, wait. I can barely keep still in my seat, willing

both of them to move. To get to their cars, to go toward the distraction. Something. Anything.

My foot taps anxiously on the floorboard of the van as I stare at him and see him wave a guy over. The second guy comes around from the other side.

"Again," I speak into the walkie and just like that, a second round goes off just as the two men move to open the gate. They take cover behind the doghouse, but the German shepherds are there, barking and going crazy. They sound vicious even from here and with a series of curses, one of the men smacks a dog over his head with the back of his gun. The yelp of the wounded animal is swallowed by the pandemonium of bangs and cracks from both the fireworks and the shots fired by men who think they're under attack.

"How many?" one yells over the supposed gunshots.

"I don't know!"

The two men scream while the sounds ricochet throughout the docks.

I can imagine what's running through their minds. They're dead men. It's too many blasts, too many guns, which means too many men for only the two of them.

I'm eerily calm watching it play out. It's only been two minutes, maybe five since we've pulled up. We don't have a lot of time before more of Mathews's men get here.

Everything's quiet, save one shepherd barking, hovering over the other dog and hollering as if he's the one in pain. The men don't look back toward the dogs or toward us, instead they stare down the road, searching for the location of the gunmen coming after them.

"Now!" I can barely hear the one man yell, the one who seems to be leading things. The one who may be high. I expect them to go down the street toward the shots, slowly making their way to gauge the threat. That's what I'd do.

He fires a few shots aimlessly, as does his partner, but they both run to the parking lot. That's when I relax slightly, feeling a smirk pull up my lips into an asymmetric grin. *They're running.*

"Again," I speak into the walkie, and the night fills with smoke as more fireworks go off. The second man is barely in the vehicle when they take off, still shooting behind him. With the squealing of their tires, we turn on the vans, revealing ourselves for the first time.

The fear in the eyes of the man shutting his door is palpable. "Go!" he screams even as their getaway car is in gear.

"Connor, once more and then back it up." I give the command. The rockets go off again and both Derrick and I hold our guns out of the window as Connor turns his van around, firing at the car as they fire recklessly at us. A bullet hits the side of the van. And then another as they drive by. The pings make my chest tighten and my blood turn ice cold each time.

With my jaw clenched tight, we keep firing as the car disappears. My gun empties first, and it only takes half a second to reload. Connor's van has already flattened the chain-link fence as he slams the van into the building, the roof of it crumbling down onto the hood. When he drives forward, it falls to the ground, but more of it collapses when he reverses again, slamming into the building and opening it wide up.

The lone German shepherd lets out a territorial bark from back in the corner of the place. Poor thing won't move away from the other. Derrick's already got the tranq and he pulls back to load it the second he steps out of the van.

"Leave them," I call out before Derrick can lift the gun. I shouldn't have said shit. But my voice was deep and I tried to disguise it.

He looks at me, standing beside the van and then back at the dogs. One's lying helpless; I don't know if he's dead or unconscious. The other isn't leaving his side.

I can see Derrick swallow, tense and uncertain before shoving the tranquilizer gun into the waist of his jeans at his back.

If he were to shoot, it'd be evidence left behind. The less we leave, the better.

Connor's already opened the back of his van and Derrick does the same to ours as I pull back the bent steel door and make my way over the rubble to see what's inside.

It's dark in the building, but the brake lights from the van give me everything we need. In the ten-by-ten-foot space, there are eight crates and nothing else.

Setup. I think the word as I walk around them. I

don't trust Wright, but so far, he told the truth. He was paid off with cash, plenty of it.

It takes a moment to pry the top off of one with my pocketknife. They're a light wood and look like something fishermen would use. Or at least that's what I imagine they're going for. I've never touched a fishing pole in my life.

Without hesitation, I crack open the one in front of me, knowing the clock is ticking away and Mathews's crew will be here soon.

Under a bed of straw is at least a dozen bricks of snow.

I heave the crate into Derrick's chest as he makes his way to me, feeling the anger consume me. It's so close. He's five miles from my turf. Setting up storage here is unacceptable.

As we haul the crates into the vans, all I can think is how I wish I'd brought gasoline, so I could light this place on fire when we're done.

Next time.

It takes only minutes with the three of us. Less than ten minutes in all to load, to get back in and take off. I keep looking in the rearview, but no one's there. When we get back to Linel Centers, we switch the plates on the vans, then park them inside to hide the one with the bullet in it. Roman will take care of that on Monday.

Moving the bricks out from the crates, we dump every last one of them down the drain. The plastic wrap cuts easily with a knife. The white powder, hundreds of thousands of dollars of it, disappears in a swirl down a filthy drain.

The large room is silent as we do it. At least at first. I've learned from each hit we do, that it takes time to cool down. It takes time to let it all turn still again.

No one says a word until we're opening up the last crate.

"First round's on me, gentlemen," Connor speaks up, breaking the silence, and takes out a flask from his car. Derrick chuckles, helping me with the last of it and takes a swig when Connor offers it. I follow suit.

Another five and we're done. It's over.

"Damn good night," Derrick comments and I nod in agreement.

Looking at the clock on the wall, an hour has passed; I broke my promise to Laura. She's definitely on her second drink by now. Fuck, I hope she didn't wait for me.

CHAPTER 6

Laura

P ICKING UP THE TWENTY OFF THE POLISHED wooden counter, I turn on my heels to face the register. My sneakers slip easily on the worn linoleum floor as I tick my blunt nails against the metal buttons until I hear the *ping* and the cash register opens.

How much shit could he have possibly gotten into in just an hour and a half last night? Every time I know he's out there, doing something—something that could get him killed—I watch the clock like it's going to have answers for me.

Like last night. I glance at the clock that never has anything for me but how long he's been gone. I stared at it for an hour and a half, making small talk in between and drinking with Roman while he watched the clock on his phone like he was waiting for something too.

I was sitting there feeling every tick of the clock squeeze my heart harder and harder when Seth sat down next to me on the leather bench in the back of the

Clubhouse, put his arm over my shoulder and kissed my jaw. He was happy and relaxed, like there's not a worry in the world.

Before I could even speak, he was making me want to thank him. *"I know I'm late, but I grabbed you the vodka you like,"* he said.

It's Grey Goose Citron and the bar was out of it. So yeah, I wanted to *thank* him.

Touching me, kissing me, giving me gifts and acting like he got stuck in traffic on the way down here.

One shot and thirty minutes later, I was laughing along with everyone else. Feeling the ease of being among friends. Even if half of them knew what Seth was doing last night and I still don't.

"Thanks for the beer," Mickey says from the far end of the bar. "Keep the change." The wrinkles around his eyes deepen when he gives me a wave and heads for the door. He's a regular. Well, a regular during the day. At night things are different; busier, louder, more… intense. Technically we're closed then and it's just a hangout. The crew—and us—aren't charged. We kick out anyone who isn't one of us due to the "private party." It's always intense, and a good time if I'm being honest, when the crew is here.

The "private parties" are what got me through so much shit.

During the day, it's just a slow old Irish bar. Lunchtime always picks up though, right about now.

"Thanks, Mick," I call out to my regular before he

can make it through the exit. The front door is old wood, dark brown except for a little black on the outside of it. Where the fire from next door caught it a few years back. The bar is in need of updating, but Seth and the guys say they like to see the memories. I get that. I like to see the memories too.

"Good luck on the test," Mick calls back to me and I flash him a smile. His bill was only twelve bucks, so I scoop eight bucks from the register and slip the cash in the back of my anatomy book that's open next to the register. I keep my finger wedged in the pages I'm reading though. I can't lose my place.

With the pen in my hand, tapping it against the notebook, I take tabs on the three remaining guests. Two are women, whispering over large pours of red wine in the back corner at a high top table. The picture frames above their heads are of the old times. Black-and-white prints from when Connor's family first came here from Ireland. Those are my favorite pictures in the bar.

The women's glasses are still relatively full, although twenty minutes ago, they were sucking the wine down like I'd given them water. The look on the brunette's face combined with a few whispers I heard tells me she most likely dumped someone, or got dumped.

Either way, they're good for another chapter of notes.

The other patron is another regular, staring up at the TV above the leather bench I sat on practically all last night. An old soccer game is on. Or a new one. I don't know and I don't care; sports aren't my thing. I assume it's an old one though, judging by how Cormac doesn't yell, "Oh, come on!" every five to ten minutes.

So, back to studying I go.

I only get two lines written in my notebook when I hear the front door open. "Welcome to the Club," I say and greet the new guest with a smile. It's automatic but it drops nearly instantly. Just like the lump that sinks down my throat before it gets stuck.

"Officer Jackson, what can I do for you?" I keep my voice upbeat and barely catch sight of Cormac taking another swig of his beer while looking over his shoulder at the cop in full uniform who just walked in. The old man eyes him, but then turns back to the television.

The officer's slick boots don't seem right in here. They look brand new with the way they're shining. Putting down the pen, I watch as he walks to the bar.

I like Jackson just fine. I always have. But I don't like him coming around because he's not one of us, and that badge on his chest could lead to problems I can't have.

I instantly wish I hadn't told Roman it was fine to take off for lunch. He hangs out here, just in case. That's what the guys tell me when I say I can manage being on shift alone when it's so slow. Just in case.

I'm pretty sure this is a *just in case* moment.

With both forearms on the bar, holding his sunglasses in one hand and releasing a deep exhale, Officer Jackson hesitates. He still hasn't said a word. I wait on pins and needles while he drags the barstool closer to him and takes a seat. He's got to be close to thirty now.

He's nice enough looking, average height although he does have a good build on him. Young for a cop, but damn did this job age him.

He's come in here before, usually to escort the drunken barflies out. A few of the older women in town don't know their limits. A couple of those few have tempers. Jackson is always the one who comes. Seth said he likes Jackson well enough. I doubt he'd like him if he knew he was here right now though.

"Everything all right?" I ask him. "Looks like you've been working out."

He huffs a quick laugh and then thanks me.

"You want a beer?" I ask him. The corners of my mouth even lift a little, thinking he's just on his lunch break. But again, the smile drops when he shakes his head. Any hope I had of this drop-in being about grabbing a bite to eat or a drink vanishes.

"You have any idea where Seth King is? I believe he's your boyfriend?"

"He *is* my boyfriend, you've got that right," I say and nod then take a step back to put down the pen in my hand. He knows damn well Seth's my boyfriend, but he asks me every time like maybe that status has changed. My back is to him as I bend down, open the small fridge and grab a cold bottle of IPA. "I think Seth said he had some errands to run today." I talk loud enough so Jackson can hear me, pop the top of the beer and turn back around to face him. "He should be here tonight, though. You need him for something?"

Taking my eyes off Jackson, I slide the beer down to Cormac who thanks me, pushing his mostly empty bottle forward.

"You're on top of it here, aren't you?" Jackson asks me.

"I can keep count of four, five... Hell, on a good day, six," I joke with him.

He laughs and leans back although his hands stay on the bar top. "You don't have any idea where he is?" he asks again, and I feel a vise grip my heart. This vise is special though; it's made of cast iron and feels like it's been sitting in the freezer the way it gives me chills and makes everything inside of me sink.

"Sorry, I don't," I answer Jackson. I'm saved by another customer walking in. I recognize her as someone who's been coming around more often lately. What the hell is her name... Cindy, maybe? She usually comes in later in the day and eyes up the guys when they first get here. She always leaves before it gets dark. Part of me thinks she wants to play with fire and she just doesn't have the balls to stay and do exactly that.

"We only have a few things available on the lunch menu," I tell her as she sidles up to a spot right between Cormac and the officer. There are two seats between her and either of the guys. "Short-staffed at the moment," I explain and pass her the paper lunch menu for the day. "We've basically got anything that can be deep-fried, but not the usual burgers."

She nods and gives a polite smile. The kind that

doesn't show any teeth. She glances at the officer too. Even with her menu lifted as if she's reading it.

"Sorry about that," I tell Officer Jackson and wait for anyone other than me to do any sort of talking.

"You're a good girl, Laura." Jackson catches me off guard with the way he says it.

Swallowing thickly, I nervously peek at Cormac, who's staring at us just like the nosy woman at the bar.

"Thank you?" I try to keep my voice even, but it shows my anxiousness.

Officer Jackson gets off his stool and talks while rapping his sunglasses on the bar. "The guys they're dealing with aren't going to let them get away with it. Get out while you can."

"I don't know—"

"I'm sure you don't," he says, cutting me off and then he tells me to have a good day before walking out.

Cormac sucking his teeth is the only thing that rips my eyes away from the closed front door.

I don't know how long I stand there staring. Hearing his last words on repeat in my head.

"He's got one thing right," Cormac tells me as I focus on stopping my hands from shaking. My back's to everyone as I pretend to be writing something down in my little notebook.

"What's that?" I manage to ask Cormac, turning to face him and leaning the small of my back against the counter.

"You are a good girl," he tells me even though he's already watching the television again.

I don't know what to say to him, so I don't respond.

"You know what you want?" I ask the woman who's still holding a menu with only five things listed on it. Cindy, or whatever the hell her name is, is frowning for the first time since she walked in.

"Not yet," she answers, and I have to try hard not to roll my eyes.

I know why Cormac thinks I'm a "good girl." It's the same reason the crew trusts me. That night is just as vivid right now as it was back then. I imagine it is for everyone who was there. That night changed everything.

I remember every detail of it as I stand with my arms across my chest, looking back at the door, and replaying that night three years ago, over in my head.

Good girl.

Cormac was there, plus everyone in Seth's crew now was there and then some. It wasn't his crew then though. And the event didn't take place here; it was a different bar. This place was empty. Connor's father had died a few weeks before. A lot of people I knew died back then. Men my father used to hang around.

It all happened at a place called Hammers. Stupid name for a bar, but it'd been around for as long as the town's existed. A little more than three years ago I was sitting at a table at that bar. I had just turned sixteen. I knew I shouldn't have been there, but when my father had to run an errand for the boss, I was supposed to wait for him at that table. My grandma rented out the spare bedroom in the house and with the new tenants upstairs, Dad didn't like me to be alone there. He was reckless with himself but a protective father. In many ways he was a shit dad, but I always knew he loved me and this was a way to show me that. Even if it was fucked up and I didn't want to be there.

I'd have a car soon. It's all I kept thinking. I hated Hammers. I hated it because if I was there, it meant my dad was out doing something he shouldn't be. For men who scared me.

The guys in the bar always told me what a good girl I was, and some of them, like Cormac, I even liked.

It didn't mean I wanted to be there though. Just the thought of that place makes my skin crawl.

Hammers was owned by the boss, Michael Vito. I knew all about him and his family. He took over when his dad died and he stirred things up. At least that's what my dad told me when I asked why so many people were getting killed. The first memories I have are of my family and friends, who used to be fine with the Vitos, acting like they were scared. Michael wanted to be feared, whereas his father was respected.

They all worked for him. I didn't want to be anywhere near that table or in that bar. But my dad told me to stay seated while he was gone, just like he had so many times before.

Vito walked in while I was sitting at my spot. It got quiet; it always did when he walked in. Another thing I hated. I had my seat and I was to keep my butt planted right where it was and do my schoolwork. My father told *me that every time he left. For years, that's what I was supposed to do. I knew Grandma would be done at the diner soon, so if he didn't get back soon, she'd find out he dropped me off at the bar again. She'd come and get me. She didn't like this place at all. She never did though.*

Thinking about Dad and Grandma makes my throat tighten.

My father didn't make the best choices in life, but he left me there because it was supposed to be safe. Everyone knew me, and everyone knew I was the daughter of a man who worked for the Vitos.

Even Michael Vito knew who I was. When he spotted me sitting there, he knew. My textbooks were open as I read Lord knows what and pretended I didn't feel his eyes on me. I pretended the bar didn't get quiet again.

I remember the sound of his heavy boots. Unlike his father, Michael carried a lot of weight to him. I remember his voice. How it was harsh when he gripped my shoulder too hard to not mean for it to hurt.

He told me to go to the back room.

The back room is where I was never supposed to go. I knew very well what happened to women who went to the back room. I could hear it. Everyone could.

Seth was there along with all of his friends. He scared the hell out of me at school. They all did. I wasn't a dork, I wasn't a cool kid, and I wasn't an athlete. I wasn't a kid who sold or did drugs either, like they were. I was just a girl who was stuck there. I knew who Seth was though, and when I looked at him, I wanted to see that it was okay and that I should listen.

Because I wanted to be a good girl. I didn't want to cause problems. Especially not for my dad who excelled at making plenty of problems for himself all on his own.

I should be a good girl and do what I was told. That's what my father said all the time. And I may have had a mouth on me, but I really did try to be good.

When I looked at Seth though, after being told to go to the back room, his expression was anything other than one of a boy who thought it would be okay if I listened. Instead his face was darkened with fear and then anger, so much anger.

"No," I blurted out without thinking. I wasn't thinking of anything other than the sounds of the girls who went into that back room. They liked it. At least I think they liked it.

But other people went into that back room too one night and they screamed. Their faces were in the paper the next morning, printed in stark black and white. Just like the pictures of the crime scene where their bodies were found.

I didn't know which option Michael meant for me, but I didn't want either of them.

"Are you telling me no?" His breath reeked of cigarettes. I'll never forget it.

"My dad told me to stay—" Before I could finish, the back of his hand whipped across my face. My neck snapped to one side and I barely stayed standing upright. I was only able to keep my footing because of the table behind me and the fact that my palms landed hard on it.

Vito yelled something in Italian, but I have no idea what it was; no one from around here is Italian. I never did understand how and why the Vitos used to run this town.

When I straightened myself to look up at him, he sneered in my face for me to get in the back room and get undressed. I don't think the others heard him, but looking at their faces, they had an idea.

"No."

He didn't slap me; he closed his fist and punched me. The burn in my nose comes back as if he's just done it, but he's gone. Long gone.

"If someone's going to show everyone else their true colors to hurt you—let them." My grandma said that once. She said sometimes people need to see. They have to look at it and swallow that harsh pill. That's all I was thinking as I lay there on the dirty floor with the taste of blood in my mouth and what I thought was a broken nose and jaw. Sometimes you have to take a hit from your enemy for them to be seen as what they are.

I did. I took the hit. And when I landed facedown and dizzy with Vito's boot pressed against my back, I didn't think the hit would do what it did.

I lay there with the coppery taste of blood in my mouth, all the while zoning in and out of semi-consciousness. My vision hazy, I thought it was the beginning of the end. I couldn't fight back; I knew I couldn't. The best *chance I had at surviving was simply being unconscious. Still, I tried to get back up, with the fear and the desperation clinging to me. Simply because I would've rather been dead or unconscious than willingly go into whatever that bitch fate had planned for me.*

The one thing I'll never know is why I didn't cry. Inside, it's all I was doing. Outside, I was willing my muscles to push me up. I wanted him to hit me again. However many times it took.

What happened next didn't last long; it felt like hours, but it was twenty minutes of brawn and bullets. I lay there crying, knowing I was going to die. I got sick once when I heard the gunshots and the yells.

I watched with horror when he was dragged to the back room. He was barely conscious, but they waited until he was with it enough in order to tell him his reign had ended. It wasn't just a brawl. It was a massacre that ended with Vito being shot in the back of the head, execution style.

The men in the bar weren't going to stand by and watch while Vito took advantage of the daughter of someone who worked for him. They weren't going to let him stomp his boot into my back while I helplessly lay on the dirty ground, flat on my stomach, which is what he was going to do after the first punch was thrown.

Even through the haze of my injuries, I saw everything from the worn wooden floors that held a stale stench of beer. I watched while a man punched Cormac in the face for shoving another man in a suit. I watched him nearly be beaten to death. It was the suits mostly, them against everyone else.

Same with Seth; he was almost strangled to death. The only reason he lived is because Derrick shot the man choking him in the back of the head. They were so close to me, the blood sprayed onto my face and neck.

Everyone lost someone that night, but it felt like we won something else.

I have to close my eyes so I don't cry at the memory.

I was still shaking, tasting vomit and blood when Seth picked me up. Half his face wasn't even recognizable; he'd been bludgeoned so badly. He walked me home and the other guys came by in twos and threes. They stayed with me until my dad got there, crying and apologizing like it was all his fault.

I begged them not to tell my grandma, but she found out. Everyone in Tremont knew what happened. They knew why things had to change.

And I was the good girl, the one who stood up against Michael Vito. Even if I didn't fight back. Even if I didn't want to be there.

Seth's father is the one who took the lead after everything went down, and he was killed along with the men who followed him within two weeks. Sometimes I wonder if his dad was still here and the crew I know today didn't make it their mission to ensure revenge, if we'd still be here. He promised me once, when he first kissed me, that he'd take me far away from this place. That was two years ago, *and here I stand, in a different bar in Tremont. Different bar, different fears.*

My phone pings at the same time the woman at the bar tells me she's ready. It takes a few minutes to do the rounds and I call back an order of fries to the cook, an old lady named Holly who only agreed to work here if she could stay in the back. She's a recovering alcoholic, but jobs in Tremont aren't growing on trees, as she explained.

I don't think anyone can tell I'm emotional. Not Holly and not Cormac. I just look pissed, maybe? Grandma used to joke that I inherited her resting bitch face. I don't know. I don't ask and I don't wait for anyone in here to say a word to me.

When I get back to my phone, I see Cami's response from me asking her to come to the appointment tomorrow with me. That's what the ping was.

What's it for? she asked me and then two minutes later when I didn't respond, she added, *Is everything all right?*

Yeah, I text back, *just that heart thing.* When I was at the doctor's two weeks ago, they said I had arrhythmia. I had a moment in the office. The stress was just getting to me, but they want me to "get it checked." Cami knows all about it. Seth too. I looked it up in detail when I got home. It's fine. It'll be fine.

What time? she asks.

3:45

I'm so sorry babe, I can't go. I have work until six but I'll keep my phone on me and I'll come by tomorrow night?

Sounds good, I text back, feeling a different kind of pain on top of the previous one that won't let go. I should have figured she'd be working on a weekday. I just wanted someone to go with me.

Cami was freaked out at first. She texts me now what she told me back then. *Don't mess with shit that deals with the heart.*

I want to tell her about Jackson; I want her to tell me anything at all to get my mind off of things.

Instead, I text her back, *Don't I know it*, and I join Cormac in watching the game.

CHAPTER 7

Seth

"THE MEET'S ALL SET UP." I'VE JUST ABOUT finished the rundown with the guys at the far left side of what will be our bar. The brown paper is laid out on the floors and the furniture is covered in cloth. The painters are coming back tomorrow since I had to kick them out early for this meet. Club Allure is coming together, piece by piece. "We've got a fight next weekend, so let's get the ring moved downstairs."

"The place isn't finished," Connor interrupts me. He's leaning against the primed walls next to Cade, who's in charge of the books, and Liam. Liam is Connor's brother and looks just like him. Especially now that they're both wearing dark jeans and dark t-shirts. Cade's the odd one in a crisp white shirt and black khakis. The rest of these guys couldn't give two shits about appearing professional. Cade comes from a different background though. He's all about numbers and left a top accounting firm to come work for me.

In another life, I'd wear suits every damn day. We don't do that here though. The men before us who wore suits destroyed any desire I had to put on tailored clothing.

"Doesn't matter," Cade speaks up, turning his head to face Connor and leaning forward so he can see him. He's the one who came to me with the idea of a fight club.

"You think anyone betting on the fights downstairs gives a shit what this floor looks like?" Derrick asks Connor, his question dripping with sarcasm.

The three of those men side by side look like they could be their own Irish crew. If things were the way they were two years ago, they'd probably be dead. The Irish didn't last too long when Michael Vito took over. The three of them are as Irish as they come. Cade comes equipped with a hint of an accent too; he's first genera-tion. With tats trailing up his right arm, it's easy to tell him apart from Liam. He's taller than Liam too, with lighter, longer hair on the top of his head. Liam looks more clean-cut. His short hair's always neatly trimmed, as is his facial hair. Even though Cade left the business world, you'd think Liam was the one who was trying to be white collar based on how they look.

"You two," I say as I gesture on both sides of Connor to the other two Irish men. "You get the say since this gig is your baby. Have it here, in the basement? Or keep it where we have been?"

"Here," Cade says, his accent peeking out. Liam

agrees with his friend. The two of them are tight, another reason they'd have been knocked off years ago. I remember telling Connor that it was on him if Cade and Liam couldn't be trusted. I have a hard time trusting people. These two are the only two guys out of the five in my crew I've brought on in the two years we've been running this shit. I don't like new blood, Connor, Derrick, Roman and I have been through everything together. We don't need anyone else. Cade and Liam can be trusted though and it's better to keep them close. So it's just my five guys and me.

That's enough for now.

"Good. I'm ready for things to start changing and the first—"

"Yo," Derrick says, cutting me off and leans his head to my right. The dark black glass for the front double doors was just installed and Laura's admiring it from where she's at the other side of the bar, still holding one door open.

"I knocked," she bellows when I call out her name to get her attention. She looks cute in a tight pair of jeans and a cropped top that shows off her stomach. Just the sight of her makes my cock twitch. My first instinct is to smile, thinking she's come to surprise me, but then I see her expression.

"Come on down," Derrick calls out to her.

"Give me a minute," I tell the guys, not liking the look on her face. It's the one she gets when she's scared but she's trying not to be. I know it well. I take a few slow steps toward her as she takes the shortest path across so she doesn't have to walk the entire distance of the place.

"It's really coming together," she says sweetly, greeting me with a quick peck and then saying hi to the guys.

"Yeah, it is. We need a few more permits," I tell her and wait. She's got both hands shoved in her pockets when she asks if there's a room we can talk in.

I don't like it. The way her shoulders are hunched in and how quietly she's talking.

"Everything all right?" I ask her as I place my hand on the small of her back and bring her around to one of the back rooms. Her doctor appointment is tomorrow. It's the first thing I think of with how she's acting. She said it wasn't a big deal. She said her heart skips sometimes and I took credit for it. Looking at her now, I feel like a jackass for making light of it. Her exact word was "harmless." She said it was harmless and the procedure was routine for diagnosis.

She better not have lied to me. Maybe I should go with her.

"Let's just talk," she answers and I pick up my pace.

The small corner room, opposite from where the guys are and what will be used for storage of unopened liquor, isn't furnished and the floors are covered with brown paper. Other than that, there's only blue painter's tape on the trim.

Laura lets out a deep exhale before I've even shut the door.

"What did you do?" she asks and her question comes out frantic. She sounds scared and it instantly makes my muscles coil, ready to beat the shit out of whoever's gotten her so worked up. But then what she says hits me.

What did I do? Relief is the first thing I feel, but then it's quickly followed by confusion.

"Whoa, hold up, what's wrong?" I ask her, taking her elbow so I can pull her in, but she pushes me away, backing up to the other side of the small room. Nervous pricks run up my arm.

"I don't like this. I don't like any of this."

With her arms crossed, she faces me from the other side of the room. I stay where I am, waiting and crossing my arms just the same.

"What did you do?" She repeats her question.

Speaking clearer this time, I ask, "What happened?"

She's stubborn. Babygirl is a stubborn broad, but she also knows I'm not going to lie to her. Which means I'm also not telling her a damn thing. It's a rule we have in the crew; it keeps the people we love out of harm's way. She doesn't need to know.

Uncrossing my arms and slipping my thumbs into my back pockets, I take a single step forward and raise my brow. *Waiting.*

A look of despair mars her face when she uncrosses her arms and confesses, "Jackson came to the bar."

A spike of rage goes through me. Just one, a blip.

"What did he say?" I ask calmly, evenly, although my voice is lower now. We have an arrangement, and for

Jackson to go behind my back and tell Laura something that's got her worked up… I'm going to have to have a word with that prick.

"He said the guys you're dealing with aren't going to let you get away with it," she says. Her voice cracks and it fucking shatters me.

Another spike of rage hits me, but this one simmers. "That seems cryptic," I tell her, keeping a poker face even though I'm already second-guessing if Jackson is talking about Mathews or if he's referring to something else. What does he know that I don't know?

Nothing.

The answer in my head is arrogant, but I can't see how he knows something I don't.

"What did you do?" Her tone pleads with me as she closes the distance between us.

The tough-girl bit falls pretty quick with her. "Please," she begs.

The second her hands reach my arms, I bring her in, holding her tight. It's what she needs, and she's quick to hold me back.

"Please, Seth," she whispers this time.

My chin rests on the top of her head as her grip on me tightens. "You're worried," I tell her, rocking her small body and staring at the blank back wall, picturing everything that happened and at what point someone would have known it was us. Jackson can't know. No one knows. He's confused or he's trying to start shit. I'll set him straight either way.

"How could I not be worried?" Laura responds with despondency.

"Jackson's bluffing, saying anything he can to get to you," I lie to her. Or maybe it's the truth. If it was though, I don't think I'd feel the way I do. Ice cold and like something bad is going to happen.

I move to hold her tighter, hating the way everything's feeling hot and numb all at once, but she breaks away, her hands on my chest as she shakes her head.

"It's not a bluff; he was worried about me." She raises her voice as she speaks but it's the emotions getting to her.

"There's no reason for you to worry," I tell her, trying to calm her down by grabbing her hands, one in each of my own.

I kiss her knuckles before telling her that I'm sorry Jackson freaked her out and that he's just a jackass.

She's not in the mood for my jokes though, if her ripping her hands away from me and pacing is any indication.

"You need to calm down," I tell her as I square my shoulders.

She asks with wide eyes, full of both hope and desperation, "Why don't you just get out of all that?" When I don't answer, she adds, "You have this bar." Like that's some sort of justification.

The bar only works because we'll do the deals here, host fights in the basement, and launder money through the alcohol sales. I struggle for a reason to give her. One day she'll realize it all. She's too smart not to piece it together. She's just messed up in the head right now and unable to see it. It's not this bar or that life. They're one and the same.

She doesn't budge right now though. "Please, give it up."

"What am I going to do?" I ask, feeling a deep crease settle in the middle of my forehead as my lips form a straight line. "Men in the life don't leave the life."

"You don't have to keep this up," she begs me, and I hate it. Every few months she does this. She can't just accept it?

"You knew who I was. There was never a question." I have to contain my frustration so I don't raise my voice.

"I thought things would change!" she yells, and I know the guys can hear. "When things got better, I thought you'd stop!"

"The guys are here." I bring up that fact to try to get her to keep her voice down. "Don't do this now." Even though it's a command, I know I'm asking her. Shit, I'd beg her not to do it in front of them.

"When are we going to do it, Seth?" she says and her voice cracks when she questions me. Her teeth sink into her bottom lip to keep it steady and the moment she wraps her arms around herself, I wrap mine around her shoulders. My chest touches her crossed arms and then her chest when she finally relaxes.

The anxiousness I feel seeing her broken down like this dims when she presses her chest against mine from her collar to her hips, and wraps her arms around me. Rubbing soothing motions up and down her back, I try to console her the best I can. Kisses in her hair, telling her it's going to be all right. I don't know what else I can do.

She knows I can't leave the guys; I can't leave the life. What the hell would I do? I don't know anything else.

That's the next step in this conversation. And then she tells me I can be anything. She believes it, too. My throat's tight when I kiss her hair again, and I breathe in deep, inhaling the smell of her shampoo. It's some floral scent.

"I love you," she whispers into my chest. I don't know if she meant for me to hear it or not, she spoke it so softly, so I don't answer. I just kiss her hair again and try to ignore that feeling in my gut that everything is all wrong.

"I hate this shit," I speak without thinking. I don't even know why I said it.

Laura takes a step back, no longer holding me and I have to straighten my expression, making sure she doesn't see anything but confidence.

"Hate what?" she asks, nearly breathlessly. Her eyes are larger, darker, swirling with a concoction of emotion that I can't quite place.

"I hate fighting," I tell her honestly. "I hate you not being happy."

"I am happy," she's quick to tell me, ignoring all of the shit that just happened so she can give me what I want. She comes to that realization at the same time that I do, and she swallows tightly. A moment passes in silence, and then another. Reaching her hands up to my collar, she stares at the stubble on my jaw as she composes herself. "I'm just scared, Seth."

"Don't be," I say, putting every ounce of reassurance I can into my tone. "I'm right here; you have nothing to be scared about."

"You're not always here, though."

I bite down hard on the tip of my tongue to keep from telling her I would be if she'd move in with me. Round and round we go. In a fucking circle.

I hate when she does this shit. Sucking in a breath, I watch her staring up at me. Wide eyed, waiting for a response and not realizing how much it pisses me off.

She's always done this, though.

Even when I first started walking her home from school. She still had the bruises and cut lip from Vito. I was busted up pretty good for a while too. It was only surface damage. That shit heals just fine. My pops took over along with his crew. If they were the first generation, we're the second for this organization. His reign didn't last long though. The Vitos weren't going to go down in a single night. Pops knew that; we all did. So someone had to keep an eye on Laura. I volunteered.

"You don't have to babysit me," I remember her telling me as I followed her down the dirt path along the field. She walked to school by herself usually, but we were engaged in an all-out war with whoever was left in Vito's

crew. No one was allowed to be alone. I stayed behind and kept my distance. Apparently it wasn't far enough for her.

"You don't have to babysit me."

"I kinda do," I called out since she was maybe six, ten feet ahead of me. It was turning to autumn and I remember how the breeze went by as she turned to face me. She may be small and meek and not wanting any of this shit, but there was so much fight in her. Still is.

She faced me, the cornfield to her back, her cheek bruised. Her bookbag fell to the crook of her arm so she could open it and pull out a sweater.

"My dad ask you to?" she asked without looking at me. She was putting all of her energy into pulling on that thin blue sweater like it was going to help her with how cold the air had just gotten. It was way too thin, but I didn't have anything for her. Shit, I was only wearing a t-shirt.

"No," I answered her and licked my bottom lip. The cut there was still pretty bad and I ran the tip of my tongue over it, remembering the weekend before. She had balls. It was more than that though that made me volunteer to watch her. She looked to me. When the moment came and she was scared, she looked at me for help. That bruise on her face? I did that to her. I might as well have. As far as I'm concerned, I'm the one who put that mark on her face. A bar full of men and it took two blows before any of us stood up to Vito. Two punches to this girl's face. Even me. Even knowing what I knew.

I never should have sat idly by. Not when it came to

her, and not when it came to all the other guys I grew up with, who Vito had knocked off one by one.

My throat got tight and I had to clear it, shoving my hands in my jean pockets and kicking the dirt as I waited for her to get moving.

"Your pops didn't ask me to, no."

"Then why?" she bit out and when I looked up, she was finally looking me in the eyes. Could she see? All the guilt I felt? I wanted to make it up to her, but I couldn't say that. When she looked at me, I should have stepped up. I shouldn't have let her be the one to say no to Vito, even if I'd never said a word to her before. She shouldn't have been the one to stand up to that man.

I couldn't speak so I just shrugged. "If you want me to go, just tell me." I implied I'd leave, but I was a lying bastard back then.

"I'd never do that," she barely whispered and pushed the words out quick, like they were toxic and crazy. Like the thought of telling me to leave would be the worst sin she'd ever make.

A moment passed, and there were so many things I wanted to say, so many things I needed to tell her, but I couldn't say any of them. So I grabbed her arm, and directed her to walk. My hand slowly moved from her elbow, down to her wrist. I didn't take her hand in mine; she did that. It took ten minutes of walking for her to do it. But she's the one who did that and I've never felt anything better.

It took her almost a year of going through turmoil

together before she caved and finally let me kiss her. Two years have passed since then, and sometimes I still feel like I did the moment she slipped her hand into mine and let me walk her home.

Laura's soft voice brings me back to the present. "Seth, I just—"

"You're scared," I say to cut her off when her plea breaks up the memory.

"Shouldn't I be?" she says, stressing the words like they're some ultimate truth.

"Come here." I give her the command with both of my arms outstretched but she shakes her head. "Hey," I say, hardening my voice and that gets her attention. "Didn't we agree I should boss you around? Or do I need to get out whips and chains?" I joke with her about that BDSM shit. It does what it should and cracks a smile on her face.

"That's only for the bedroom," she tells me and rolls her eyes, but her soft smile is still there. I motion for her to come to me and she does. Resting her head on my shoulder even though she's focused on twirling the ends of her hair around her fingers.

"You're scared," I tell her again. She's quiet but I know she's listening because her motions stop. "Steven Jackson knows some things, but not everything. Maybe he is scared for you, maybe he thinks something happened. I don't know, but I can tell you," I pause to wrap my hand around the nape of her neck and wait for her to look at me before continuing, "he doesn't know shit."

I don't know if it's a lie or the truth, but her gaze already softens with relief. Her pouty lips drop open slightly, but I keep talking before she can say anything.

"He doesn't know what he's talking about because we don't tell him everything. Only little things he needs to know to keep him off our back." Her eyes search mine and I don't know what she'll find after that half-truth leaves me.

"If something was wrong, or if you were in danger, you know I'd hide you away." I run my hand through her hair as I add, "I'd probably lock you up in that safe at the house." I grin at the ridiculousness and she lets out a broken laugh and then sniffles.

I let a minute pass, just rocking her, allowing her the moment she needs to realize Jackson isn't the be-all and end-all. I am.

"I'm sorry he got you all worked up and upset," I tell her and kiss the crown of her head.

"I'm sorry I let him," she says. Her apology is quiet, and I hate it. Before I've even straightened my spine to stand upright, she's coming at me, kissing me and wrapping her hands around my shoulders to keep me lowered for her.

Her lips are hot, and her tongue is greedy. Everything inside of me simmers. "Greedy girl," I groan against her lips when she finally pulls away.

My right hand has already drifted to her ass, keeping her hip pressed against my thigh. My left is roaming, feeling curves I know so well and wanting to sear her skin, branding it with my touch to make sure she still belongs to me.

"Seth," she murmurs. The combination of tearstained cheeks and lust in her eyes makes me hard as stone for her. "I love you," she tells me. "I hope the guys didn't hear," she adds before she takes another breath. She's quick to do that. To deny me the opportunity to say it back. She's afraid I won't. I get it. I don't mind it either. She likes to protect herself however she can.

"I'm sure they did," I answer her and then reach behind me to the doorknob, making sure it's locked. The click is in time with the thump in my chest. "They aren't going to hear you yell at me anymore though," I tell her and unbutton my pants.

Laura's thighs clench as she stands there, in a ten-by-ten-foot room with me and nowhere to hide. Desire dances in her eyes.

"We can't," she hisses, accompanied by the zip of my pants being undone.

"If they can hear you yell at me, they can hear me fucking you, so you better be quiet."

My sweet innocent girl gasps and it thrills me. I love that I can still surprise her. "Don't let them hear you," I command her as I take a step forward, kicking off my jeans and sliding down my drawers as I go. She takes a step back until her shoulders hit the wall, as if she can escape me. As if she'd want to. "I want them to hear all the banging from me fucking your brains out against this wall. Not you moaning my name. Just this." Splaying my hand on the drywall above her head, I slap my hand hard once against the wall. I lean my lips to the shell of her ear and say, "You need to be quiet. Do you hear me?"

My cock is already leaking precum at the thought of being inside of her and everything being right again. Her small hand reaches out between us and she rubs the moisture over the head of my dick, making me groan. Dropping my lips to the crook of her neck, I kiss and suck and nibble while she strokes me until I've had enough.

It takes everything I have to step back and tell her to strip down. I want her ass completely naked. Both of us. Our clothes are nothing but puddles of fabric on the floor. Before I lift her up, I run my fingers between her slick folds, teasing her, rubbing her sweet nub and testing her ability to be quiet. Her nails dig into my shoulder as she bites down on her lip. Her head slams against the wall as she rocks herself on my hand. She's breathing too heavily, making too much noise.

I don't give a shit though. It wouldn't be the first time my crew caught us going at it. They know to get the hell away and leave us alone.

With a hand on each of her ass cheeks, I lift her up and she wraps her legs around my waist. "Bite my shoulder," I demand, and she does it instantly. It's a good thing she doesn't hesitate, because I slam into her out of pure unadulterated need. My thrusts are primal and the harder she bites me, the harder I fuck her. My body is covered in a cold sweat and hers is hot to the touch on every inch. I take her like we both need, and I have no regrets about that.

No fucking regrets. Not anymore.

CHAPTER 8

Laura

I CAN'T EVEN CROSS MY LEGS; I'M SO SORE. SETH HAS some sort of magic over me. I don't know what it is. The moment I'm in his vicinity, I'm a puppet for him. Whatever he commands, I do. Whatever he tells me, I believe. My body bends to his and I love it.

It does terrify a small piece of me, though. That little voice is quiet right now, sated by what happened in the back room last night.

And then again when Seth met me at his place and took me to bed.

That second time reminded me of our first time. I keep comparing the two and I find nothing identical. Back then when I first gave into Seth years ago, the temptation to touch him, the urge to let him do whatever he wanted to me—I had never experienced it with anyone else. I knew nothing, except that I wanted him to finally touch me, to have me like I'd been fantasizing about. It would have happened sooner if my dad hadn't died shortly after Seth started hovering over me. He was my protector for nearly a year before I kissed him.

I remember being up on my tiptoes, my hand pressed against his chest and I kissed him as though I had done it a thousand times before. And I had in my mind. Every time he opened the door for me. Every time his fingers brushed against mine when we walked. Every time he laughed at the bar and with the rough cadence his hand landed on my thigh and stayed there. In the very forefront of my mind I leaned into him and kissed him, thousands of times or more. So that day, after having a drink and feeling the buzz of both intoxication and lust, I planted my lips directly onto his.

I never imagined the groan of satisfaction. That deep, masculine sound was unexpected and a pleasant surprise that travelled down to my belly, and then further. His rough hands gripped my hips and he lifted me up, keeping his lips on mine, never breaking the heated embrace.

Last night was slow and leisurely; that first night was a rush of primitive need. He couldn't take my clothes off fast enough, until my bare back was on the table and my ass was hanging off. I'd have been mortified if he hadn't dipped his head to my breasts and sucked, nipped and ravished every inch of my flesh. How could I be embarrassed by my body when he worshipped it the first glance he got?

I was naked while he was still clothed. Again, it's a

difference. Last night was slow, relaxing, and he stripped first, then he took his time peeling my clothes off.

"I'll go slow," he whispered at the crook of my neck when he had finally made it to that moment. The moment when I was no longer a virgin. I remember how hot I felt. How suffocating those prolonged seconds were between knowing it was going to happen, and it finally happening.

"I don't want you to go slow," I told him, my mind clear and my desire evident. "I want you."

In one swift stroke he took me, hard and unabashed. He watched me as my eyes widened; he never stopped watching between heated kisses.

"I'll make sure you love it," he promised as he pounded into me with reckless abandon and I don't know for certain if the promise was for me or for him.

My thighs tighten and I can still feel him. That night I knew I could never go back. I wasn't sure if he could go back to pretending the attraction wasn't there. He made damn sure I knew the next day when he took me into the bar and kissed me in front of everyone. There was never any "going back" with Seth.

When my phone buzzes in my hand, I instinctively jump from my seat in the waiting room and then hiss at the slight pain that throbs between my legs. It's a good ache, but it's embarrassing as fuck when the receptionist eyes me from behind the glass divider. Like I'm some kind of nuisance. I don't want to be here anymore than she wants me here.

I want to be a nurse; I don't want to be a patient. I hate being a patient. Mostly because of insurance.

I've already got my clipboard of paperwork filled out. Now I just wait in this room, sitting in one of the chairs that look like they're from the '80s while a cooking show plays in the upper right corner on a tiny little TV.

I check the text I received, thinking it might be from Seth, but it's not. *Tell me something good.*

Cami's text makes me smile.

No news yet, I'm waiting to be seen. YOU tell me something good. I'm eager for her to distract me. I want to know all about what she and Derrick did last night. I feel like I'm in on the details because she told me, but Derrick didn't tell Seth. I know because last night Seth told me he thinks that Derrick's seeing someone seriously.

You have to tell me what they say. As I read the text Cami sent back, a little disappointed that it's not full of juicy details, an elderly woman in an oversized t-shirt comes into the waiting room from the doctor's side and then leaves through the front doors. I glance at the woman at the front desk, wondering if this means it's my turn, but nope, nothing yet.

Tap, tap, tap, my shoe is at war with the wooden leg of my chair.

Cami texts me again and I nearly shriek in the room. The gasp is certainly audible and when I look at the receptionist, she's looking at me disapprovingly. Fucking hell. This isn't the library.

Giving her a tight smile, I return to my phone and read the text again.

Derrick and I slept together last night.

I've known Cami for half a decade. She's slept with three men in her life before last night. Derrick is the fourth. All three were young love... for Cami. The guys told her they loved her, fucked her, and moved on. Derrick won't do that. I know he won't. He wouldn't have touched her if he didn't want more from her. He knows she means a lot to me. He told Cami that's why he didn't make a move sooner. He was afraid of getting into trouble with "the boss," meaning Seth.

So this is the end of 'let's take it slow'? I ask her.

I have to wait a few minutes to get a response, and in the meantime, I text her about half a dozen times: *How was it? How big is he? Where did it happen?*

It's practically an interview when she finally texts back.

He told the guys last night he was into me. He said he claimed me, like the guys used to do at the Clubhouse, you know? His dad and them.

She rambles in her messages, sending them in chunks. And all the while my heart does a little flip for her. But also for me. Seth was fucking with me. Maybe he wanted to see if I knew. Dammit, I'm more disappointed than I should be that I'm not in on a secret Seth doesn't know of.

He said if I'm with him, we're exclusive. That he'll be out late some nights, but it's for work. He said I can't ask questions and I have to trust him. He told me that it's hard for some girls to trust like that and he asked me if I could.

And you said yes? Right? I text back with my questions even though I already know she did. Cami knows everything I've been through with Seth. Late nights after we've had fights are the worst. It's easy to think he's just avoiding me, that he's off somewhere trying to get me—and our fight—off of his mind.

Those nights, I called Cami.

She'd come over or stay with me on the phone, easing my worries. Somewhere deep down, I knew Seth wasn't going to leave me, but it didn't make the thoughts in my head stop. We've had three big fights, all about the stupid shit he does and how we can get out of it. All three times, I watched that clock. All three times, he eventually came home, then sat next to me like he belonged there. Even if I wasn't talking to him when he left. All three times, I kissed him hard, loving that he made the choice to come back to me.

He's a man who doesn't leave. All of the guys in the crew are the same. Derrick will be to Cami what Seth is to me; I know it.

She didn't grow up in the life, but she gets it. Her dad was a truck driver and not around a lot. Maybe that's why it's easier for her? I don't know. But she stays calm in the storm. Derrick's lucky to have that.

My phone pings.

I told him to shut up and kiss me. He wasn't telling me anything I didn't already know.

This time I do squeal and I don't bother to look up at the receptionist. She can deal with it.

"Laura Roth?" a doctor calls out into the room, looking at a clipboard and lifting the papers before looking up to see me. The doctor looks young at first, but then I see the age around her eyes and mouth. She's done up with dangling earrings, her brunette hair piled high in a bun, and a black dress under the professional white coat.

I wave. Like an idiot. I'll blame it on being caught off guard by Cami's last text.

"Come on back." Her voice is calming yet chipper as she holds open the door and leads the way to whatever room we're going to. "I'm Dr. June. It's nice to meet you." She's polite and confident. I find myself making up stories about her on the way through the hall.

I wonder if she has a date after work. Or maybe it was a lunch date. She's even wearing heels and that seems like a bold choice. I've already picked out the white sneakers I want to wear when I'm a nurse.

"Have a seat," Dr. June says as she directs me to a blue examination table with vinyl upholstery that seems cheap but is probably easy to clean. It's covered by a sheet of white paper that crinkles when I sit down.

"So I see here you were at your gynecologist and she identified what she believes to be a potential arrhythmia?"

I nod my head, remembering that day and a certain feeling in particular. I'm experiencing it again right now, this draining of everything inside of me right to the pit of my stomach.

"Can you tell me when you first experienced these symptoms?"

I move my gaze from her to the stark sink and the clear canisters filled with odd-shaped swabs. "I um—" I stop speaking to clear my throat. "I wouldn't have known if I hadn't been there, so I don't really know."

"The chart indicates you grabbed your chest and seemed to struggle to breathe." I can hear the paper fall as Dr. June drops the clipboard to her lap. "Is that a normal occurrence?"

"I'd just found out." It hurts all over again. "I went in because I was bleeding, and I'd just found out that I miscarried. I didn't even know I was two months along." My eyes prick with tears, but I keep them back. "I didn't know I was pregnant. ... So, no, it's not a normal occurrence. I was just reacting to the situation."

"I can understand that," Dr. June says and nods, trying to ease the thick tension. I hate this room. I hate being the one sitting on this table.

She asks me the same questions the gynecologist did. If I've felt fatigued, light-headed, or experienced any rapid heartbeat and shortness of breath in the last six months. All of them are a yes, but it's because of Seth and the shit he puts me through, so I lie, which I know I shouldn't do, and tell her no.

"I've already answered these for the other doctor, my gynecologist," I say and cut her off from asking more questions, feeling like this is all déjà vu.

103

"I know, but for the tests we have to conduct, we have to do this at our facilities." Paperwork. Legalities.

"I understand."

"So today, I'm going to listen to your heart and do a checkup of sorts. We're also going to do an echocardiogram to take a look at what's going on physically. It's an ultrasound ..." Her voice drones on as she lists what she has planned for me and her reasoning for the tests. I've already read up on it, so I'm ready. Her stethoscope is cold as she listens to my heartbeat, occasionally pausing to tell me to breathe in deep.

All the while, I think about moments like this that I may face as a nurse. With me on the other side of things. If there's ever a woman talking about her miscarriage and on the brink of tears, I promise myself not to keep a smile plastered on my face and tell her that I understand.

You can never understand what anyone else's pain is like. She doesn't know Seth told me he wanted kids. And that I told him I didn't; there was too much going on.

I was already pregnant when I told him that. I put that out there into the universe, not knowing I was already carrying the baby Seth wanted. I practically asked fate to take that baby away from me. From us.

I'll never forgive myself for speaking those words out loud. For even thinking them. I wish I could take it back. I would if I could. You're never ready for a baby.

"You may want to ask someone to go with you." Dr. June's suggestion brings me back to the present.

"For the stress test?" I clarify, shifting and making

the paper crinkle under me. I was barely listening to her telling me I'll have to come back in next week.

"Yes. It's just a treadmill and I don't think you'll have any problems, but it may be comforting to have someone with you."

I'm grateful the stethoscope is nowhere near me, suddenly worried that she can hear just how battered my heart feels. I don't want to lie to her even more than I already have, so I don't tell her I asked the only two people I have to come today and neither of them could.

CHAPTER 9

Seth

FROM THE PARKING LOT OF THE OLD GAS STATION, you could throw a stone and hit a car on the highway. It's that damn close. It's loud too as the three of us huddle for this meet.

Behind me is the old worn-out sign, bleached by the sun but you can still read *Gas and Convenience Store*. Under it is my crew. Roman, Connor and Liam are talking about something. I don't know what. I can't hear shit with the highway here.

Derrick looks with me, and then tells me, "Should be simple." Maybe he thinks he needs to ease my concerns, so I nod. "Yeah," I respond.

I can't shake this feeling in my gut though. Ever since Laura came home from the doctor's two nights ago, something feels off. Not just with her, but with work too.

It's like someone's watching me. A gust of wind passes, and I the feeling comes over me again. I don't like it.

Leroy holds out his hand for a shake before saying a word. His crew's behind him like mine is, at a distance and leaning against a black sedan. His grip is strong and he looks me in the eyes as he says, "I'm looking forward to doing more business with you fellas."

I can see in my periphery that Derrick's lips kick up in an asymmetrical grin at "fellas."

Leroy's from down south and he needs shipments coming in. We can provide that. We have in the past, but these should be steady, or so he claims. Shipments come into the dock, we collect, we deliver. Like Derrick said, *should be simple.*

"You know our take," I tell him and then my gaze is pulled past Leroy when one of his crew reaches behind him. My hand burns with the need to go for my gun when I see the quick motion, but the guy is just reaching for a smoke. With the cigarette in his mouth, he takes out a lighter from his back pocket and passes it to the guy next to him. "Fifteen percent," I tell Leroy, keeping my expression easy, even though adrenaline is scorching through me.

I know you need trust in these relationships. At least trust that they need the partnership and can't afford to fuck you over. I have that with Leroy. I have for a year now although this proposition is new. I just can't shake this feeling though.

Not everyone is an enemy. But damn does it feel like they are sometimes.

Leroy shifts his focus to Derrick, who's silent. The

gravel under his feet crunches noisily while we wait. "What if I increase the load, can your boys handle that?" he asks me, and I nod.

"We got it covered."

Another second passes. "If I increase the product per shipment, seems like it should be dropped to ten percent, doesn't it?"

"How's that?" Derrick pipes up. I roll out my right shoulder, watching Leroy's men talking. A freight truck rushes by on the highway above them and two of them turn to look. It's not a high-tension situation, but negotiations at the last minute aren't welcome.

"More product, more money, but you're still only doing one run," he explains to Derrick.

"We agreed on fifteen," I tell him.

Leroy puts both of his hands up, a move that makes the men behind him still, their eyes focused solely on us now. *Thump, thump* my heart pounds and the back of my neck pricks. His hands are lowered as quickly as they went up, and his men settle. They're watching closely now though.

"I got a call yesterday. I may have more product than I thought. Terms for me have changed," Leroy says then sniffs and thumbs the tip of his nose. "Like I said, it's more product, more money, still one shipment. Ten percent of this load is more than fifteen percent of the previous."

"How much more?" I ask him.

"Forty."

HARD TO LOVE

Forty thousand.

I still hesitate and he adds, "How long have we been working together? Two years now? I don't want to work with anyone else. You're my guy."

Another truck goes by as I take in what he's saying. I don't like changing arrangements.

"We've got the cash in the car," he says. As he moves to call over one of the guys, I see a familiar car pull up to the gas station. It's an old, light blue Mustang. The paint is worn out, but I think Jackson likes it that way.

"We got company," I murmur and nod my head for Leroy to see.

"He's not one of yours?" Leroy's brow arches.

"We have him contained, but he doesn't get a paycheck," I explain.

"No exchange then?" he questions. I eye Jackson, parked at a pump and sitting there, not even bothering to get gas. Fucker.

"No, we still exchange. We have a deal at twelve percent because it's more work for us, more heat too if anything happens." I hold out my hand for Leroy.

It takes a few seconds, but he agrees and his handshake is just as firm as it was when he first pulled up. "It's always nice doing business with you."

Turning to Derrick, I tell him to get the details and the cash—all twelve percent of it. "I'll take care of this."

"Until next time," Leroy says, giving me a nod as I walk off. Dust kicks up from the parking lot as I walk the twenty feet or so over to Jackson.

109

The highway's louder at the front of the store than on the side where the parking lot is. A car beeps on the bypass above, quick and short, but in multiple successions and it aggravates me just as much as the sight of Jackson does right now.

I could fucking snarl, remembering how he got into Laura's head.

It takes everything in me not to grab him by his throat and slam him up against his car. The only reason I don't do it is because of the deal going on behind me. If Leroy thinks I'm in over my head with the cops, he could back out. Shit, I would if it were me, but we need this cash. We need everything we have right now. The twelve percent from Leroy with a higher take? That's good for us. I probably would have taken the ten given it's still one run. A steady cash flow is what we need while we get the bar up and running.

With my jaw clenched, I stare down at Jackson. My shoulders are tense and I breathe in the dusty air just to keep from screaming at this asshole.

"Come to tell me you're worried for me?" I raise my voice as I speak so he can hear, not changing the expression on my face.

"Worried for you?" Jackson keeps his door open, standing with it between him and me and that makes me uneasy. I want his hands where I can see them. Which is ironic, given who he is.

"Get out and shut the door," I demand and he cocks his head, staring at me like this is a showdown.

"You want to have this conversation while I'm thinking you're hiding a gun between the two of us?" I question him and that gets him moving. The door shuts as another round of cars rushes behind us, below us. We're surrounded by activity.

Jackson's my height and my build. Ever since we were kids, we were built the same. At least physically. Mentally, we were always opposites.

Before he's finished taking the two steps it takes to get close enough to talk, I tell him, "Don't ever go to Laura again." The threat in my voice is clear as day. I don't do subtleties when it comes to her.

Jackson isn't fazed. It should piss me off, but instead I find myself questioning things.

"She deserved a heads-up and so do you, which is why I'm here."

"You leave her to me," I tell him again, gritting the words out between my teeth.

"A moment of weakness," he says and then glances at the pavement before looking me in the eyes. "I apologize."

My muscles twitch; my back feels like it's tighter than a coiled rope ready to split and unravel.

"Wright is a snitch," Jackson says, changing the subject. My mind is still on Laura, still on the stress he caused her. Hearing Wright's name though, the source of our intel and a lower-level mule for Mathews, catches my attention.

"If he snitched to us, you don't think he told Mathews?" Jackson questions me.

"Told you what?"

"You stole half a mil in product—at cost." He emphasizes cost and it takes a lot for me to stay calm in this moment. I have to keep my voice low and even, show no emotion. Leroy's men are watching.

With that in mind, I look over my shoulder. Derrick's at the corner of the store where I can see him. The car's parked in the back. I imagine he's having Roman do the bitch work of moving the cash from one car to the other. As long as Derrick's in view, I know everything's going as planned.

Other than what Jackson just told me. *Wright's a snitch.*

"It wasn't us and I don't know what you're talking about."

Jackson shakes his head and sucks his teeth. "Don't do that to me. Not with all the shit I've covered up for you. Don't fucking do that to me." I don't expect the anger, or the hurt. That's what it is in the way he looks at me with his nostrils flared. He's hurt.

"We've known about them coming down here. We grabbed Wright. We had him spilling everything. Then you go and fuck with them?" Contempt laces his last line.

Clenching my fist and cracking my knuckles with my thumb, I take a moment. Letting this information sink in as I watch Leroy and Derrick shake hands before our respective crews part ways. Mine stays where they are, waiting for me while Leroy and his men take off in two vehicles, one after the other. Jackson and I both watch in silence.

"These guys like Mathews don't just get angry; they make examples of the people who steal from them."

"And you were going to stop him?" I question him. I remember when we were just kids. This is a small town and I knew all the neighborhood kids. We'd play cops and robbers back then. He was always the cop and I was always the robber. The "bang" of our toy guns didn't come with the same kick back it comes with now.

"We were getting the intel we needed to get the feds involved."

"Are they?" I ask him.

"Are they what?"

"Involved?"

His gaze drops and I already have my answer. No. Mathews must not be big enough. Either that or Wright didn't give them good enough intel.

"What do you want from me?" I ask Jackson, wanting this conversation to be over so I can figure out how we're going to handle this.

"Come in—get protection. Especially for Laura. It doesn't have to be like this."

Protection? I scoff at the very idea that Jackson would be bringing this shit up. "You remember what it was like. It *does* have to be like this."

"This is too much. They're too big. The collateral—"

"Is my problem," I say, cutting him off. "I can handle this."

His expression falls when I raise my voice. I can feel the words still ringing in my throat long after they're spoken.

Opening his car door, he tells me grimly, "Then, at least I warned you. You know where I am if you change your mind."

CHAPTER 10

Laura

I HEAR SETH BEFORE HE SAYS A WORD TO ME. THE door isn't shut quietly; it's practically slammed. Gripping the edge of my nightgown, for a moment I wonder if it's him or someone else since it was shut so hard. But then I hear the jingle of the keys as they hit the bowl we keep in the kitchen. It's an old ceramic bowl my grandma gave me. At least he didn't throw the keys in there hard. I'd have to kick his ass if he ever broke it.

I must have dozed off; the clock on the nightstand tells me it's nearly nine. When I check my phone, still hearing Seth slamming what sounds like the fridge door, I see a handful of messages Cami sent. Shit, we were supposed to go out. She gathered, in the series of texts I'm reading, that I forgot or that I was busy.

Writing her a quick reply, I tell her I'm sorry. I never miss our dates. Ever. I feel like complete shit that I fell asleep.

I answer the two questions she asked me as well.

They're questions about birth control. I promise in the next message I'll make it up to her.

She's quick to tell me it's okay. She's already replaced our date with one with Derrick.

I would feel relief, but Seth's still out there.

There's a little nagging piece inside of me. Digging and clawing, making me feel that something really is wrong. It heats my skin; it sickens my stomach. It tells me to worry. This is what he does when I'm not looking. He bangs shit around and lets out his stress that way.

As I'm walking in the hallway, not trying to be quiet, but quiet nonetheless, I hear the slam of his fist on the counter. My heart jolts in my chest, seizing for a moment until I peek out from the threshold and see my towering man hunched over, both forearms resting on the counter, his head laying between them. His broad shoulders stretch the white t-shirt he's wearing tight over his muscular back. Every muscle ripples as he breathes in deep in what looks like an attempt to calm himself.

"Everything okay?" I ask a little quieter than I'd planned, feeling that aching whisper scream inside. My fingers twitch with the need to hold him, to come up behind him and comfort Seth as he's done for me so many times. But I wait.

Some nights are bad and he doesn't like to be touched then. Not when he first gets home. Maybe it's because he wanted to throw shit around like he is now, but he couldn't because I was home.

He lifts his gaze to me and instantly softens. His

exhale is short as he stands up straighter, running his hand over the back of his head. "Sorry, Babygirl. I didn't know you were home. Thought Cami and you were going out?"

Seth clears his throat and then opens his arms, urging me to come over to him. I don't waste any time molding myself to the side of his body, feeling his heat. With one arm around my waist, he hugs me back and then lifts the beer on the counter to his lips with his free hand.

"You okay?" I ask once the glass clinks on the counter, noting he takes his time with the swig, probably to get his thoughts in order.

"Fine," he breathes out although stress is prominent in his answer. "How did the studying go?" he asks me, changing the subject. He does that a lot, but I can still see the torment that clings to him. Maybe he thinks he hides it well, but he doesn't.

"So you don't want to talk?" I ask him, hoping maybe all he needs is a push.

All he gives me is a weak smile though. I already knew he wouldn't confide in me. It's just not who he is. Grabbing both of his hands and making him leave the beer on the counter, I tell him to come with me.

His fingers barely grip mine until I give his hand a squeeze.

"You all right?" he asks and a new worry rips through his expression. It's fresh, not tired. And fear, not stress.

I have to laugh a little when I answer him, "I'm better than you are." I'm still walking him to the sofa in the living room when he gives me a huff of a masculine laugh in response. Seth's house is larger than my grandma's. Nicer in a lot of ways simply because it's new and in an up-and-coming part of town. The sofa though, it's my favorite. The entire living room really. Probably because I picked out every piece.

The sofa is a soft cream chenille with a pale blue paisley pattern on the outsides of the armrests and all the way around the back of it. When I picked it out, I was thinking of myself and thought for sure Seth would say no. Instead, he told me to get whatever I wanted to go with it. So I got a thick, plush royal blue rug to go with the sofa, covering the hardwood floors, solely so I could get on my knees like I'm doing now, unbuckling his pants and helping Seth relax.

I can give him this. Freely. He gives me so much and never asks for a damn thing. So this? I can give him this.

He spears his hand through my hair as the sound of the zipper mixes with my faint moan.

"Laura," Seth protests weakly and my response is to grip his jeans in both my hands, ripping his pants down as I stare up into his heated gaze. He's already hardening. I can see his length get stiffer by the second through the thin fabric of his boxer briefs.

"Sit down." I give him the firm command while keeping our eyes locked, and he smirks at me. From this angle, he's even more handsome, which doesn't make any sense. He's just towering over me. Maybe it's the rough stubble, the way he smiles, or the lust in his eyes. But my heart does that little pitter-patter, the beat that's out of rhythm. Maybe it really is all because of him. *He makes my heart skip a beat.*

"Let me do what I want to you," I whisper and inch my fingers up to the waistband of his boxer briefs. His hand is still in my hair, and he scratches his blunt nails against my scalp before wrapping my hair around his wrist. Pulling my head back, I'm forced to look at him, rather than his hardening cock that's barely contained by the thin fabric in front of my face. He doesn't pull hard, not enough to give me any pain, but it's authoritative.

I think for a moment he's going to say something; his gaze is so penetrating and he stares for so long. All the while, my core heats, my heart flutters, and I can barely breathe.

Seth releases me without a word, letting me strip him down, dropping slowly to the sofa, spreading his strong legs wide for me.

His cock is ready, standing tall when I reach out and stroke him. My fingers nearly don't wrap around the entire thing. I run my thumb up one of the thick veins all the way to his head. Spreading a bead of precum over the velvety top of him, I almost lick my lips.

"I like it when you blush like that," he murmurs. Looking up at him, I hold his gaze as I lean forward and let the tip of my tongue slip through his slit while holding him with both hands to keep him where I want him. He hisses and the *S* sinks deep into my heat, forcing me to clench around nothing.

I wrap my mouth around the head of his cock and hum a sweet moan as I taste the saltiness of what little cum is there. Opening my jaw as far as I can, I sink down his length and feel his smooth skin massage my lips as I bob. It's only a tease, only to get a little moisture on his cock. Releasing him with a pop, I look back up at Seth, whose lips are parted as he breathes ever so slowly. His hips thrust in my hand the next time I lean down, teasing his head with a gentle suck.

I could worship his cock like this for hours, but he doesn't let me.

A squeal leaves me when he reaches down, grabbing me by the hips to sit in his lap. "Seth!" I object, but that doesn't stop him from ripping my nightgown over my head. I'm mid-laugh when his open-mouth kiss lands on the dip in my throat. The giddiness in my voice is quick to morph to a strangled moan when he touches me. His hands grip my flesh, and his mouth devours my sensitized skin.

I anticipate him maneuvering me onto my back upon the sofa, with him on top. That's how he likes it most of the time. But he doesn't. Instead he places my back to his chest, still kissing my neck, and spreads my legs so my thighs are resting over his.

"Seth," I moan as his cock presses against my folds. The head slips against my clit and I writhe against him, my breath hitching.

He's not merciful as he pushes himself inside of me with a single stroke. My back arches, and my front feels cold without him here. Seth keeps my neck at his lips by gripping my throat with his hand. I'm staring at the ceiling, wide eyed, feeling the sweet stretch that lingers with pain when his other hand meets my throbbing clit.

He's relentless as he strums my swollen nub and pistons his hips up to fuck me just like this. My screams of pleasure are as ruthless as his touch. He doesn't stop until my throat is sore, my limbs are trembling and I've orgasmed more times than I can keep count.

CHAPTER 11

Seth

THERE ARE TWO PLATFORM STAGES IN THE basement of Club Allure. The one in the center, a sixteen-by-twenty-foot rectangle, has bright lights shining down on it. They're highlighting two men as they circle each other. The drop is only two feet if one of the hulking men falls off. It's the platform of a professional boxing ring, minus the ropes. It looks like Jameson might fall off the edge. The blood from the cut above his eye is dripping down his face and he can barely keep up with protecting his body with his fists, let alone keep the blood from blinding him.

If he falls, he's still fair game. Just harder for every-one else to see the ass beating he'll take. Judging by the cheers and the frown on Cade's face, this match isn't an upset. There are four more after it though, and regardless of how this match turns out, these men will keep betting. For the thrill, for the entertainment. For the addiction of being a part of something so primitive. All of which is good for us. We haven't had a fight yet that didn't line our pockets. This is the first one down here; the first of many.

In front of where Derrick and Liam are standing on top of the second stage, the one against the back wall, I approach Fletcher. Derrick and Liam are watching it all go down while Cade takes the bets. At least sixty bodies form a swarm around the ring, filling the room with their cheers and yells. It's all white noise. The real money is made away from the lights, in the shadows of the room while surrounded by the chaos.

With men like Fletcher. He runs things up north of here. He has for years and when shit got rough the first year of taking Tremont back from Vito's men who wanted it just as much as we did, Fletcher took our side.

Back then, he said he was rooting for the underdogs. I wonder if he bet on Jameson tonight.

"King," Fletcher greets me and I grip his hand firmly, keeping my gaze on anything but his pocket square. He always wears a suit I can't stand.

Ostentatious is one way to describe the pale blue suit that's wrapped around his body in a slim fit. With the yellow patterned handkerchief tucked in his pocket, garish is the word I'd use for this one. Fletcher is flashy, from his heavy gold watch to the diamond stud in his ear. His look comes outfitted with a lit cigar. Money talks, but the wealth he has, he decides to make scream. I may not prefer his attire, but he's just the man I want to do business with tonight.

"Good to see you, Fletcher."

"Your bar is coming together nicely," he says, starting with small talk. Upstairs isn't finished, and it won't be for another few weeks or more. I want it perfect when we open the doors to the public. Down here is just fine. No furniture, nothing that can be stained with the blood that will most certainly be spilled. These heathens would be fine with cardboard boxes.

"Thanks. I heard you're building one uptown?" I question him and he shrugs.

"Not like this," he says.

"Wasn't asking because I'm worried about competition," I say to reassure the worried look on his face.

He huffs from his nose before straightening the gaudy handkerchief. "I just want you to hear it from me. I'd never step on your toes."

"Likewise," I say with a nod and move on to business. "The next shipment has been moved up a week. Leroy has extra product, and he's happy for me to hand it on over to you."

"You want me to cut out Mathews?" Fletcher questions, a glint in his eye. He's had to deal with Mathews because there was no one else. It's what led to that fucker getting closer to Tremont. This is one more blow to Mathews while giving me favor with both Leroy and Fletcher. It's a win on all sides and both of them know it.

If I need an ally against Mathews, Fletcher is my man.

"Who's that?" I ask with a smirk and he lets out a

bellow of a laugh. Fletcher sells what Mathews sells. All the heavy shit. Pushing Mathews back by destroying his stash only helps Fletcher keep his territory. *Stick with the devil you know*, comes to mind when I think about the last conversation Fletcher and I had.

"Know what I love about you?" he asks me, wrapping an arm around my shoulders. "You treat your friends well."

I give him a tight smile and nod. "I take it you're happy to not have to rely on the man cutting into your turf?"

"This last week has been less bloody," he tells me with a seriousness that chills my spine. "I want to keep it that way."

"It's been coming to that. A war on the streets."

Fletcher nods and says, "That's what happens when a new dealer moves in."

"I heard he's moving out," I'm quick to comment as Fletcher lights up a cigarette. He takes a long puff and exhales as the men surrounding the stage to our right, let out the kind of roar that comes with disbelief. Looks like Jameson's coming back. That's what happens with the Irish. You can't count them out until they've hit the ground.

"He can sell his shit elsewhere," Fletcher says, practically spitting the words out. "It was a mistake to ever buy from him... This Leroy... he's all right?"

"Been with him for a while, he's better than all right."

"What have you been buying, though?" Fletcher

questions me and I don't like it. "That soft shit isn't the same type of deal."

I level him with a hard stare. "You don't have to worry about Leroy."

He's slow to nod, then drags on his cigar before saying, "Tremont has some good shit. The pot, the coke, the E…. but when are you going to expand, Young Buck?"

Young Buck. I hate the nickname he has for me even more than the suit I'm currently forced to look at.

"We're stable, controlled, that's how I like it," I tell him and then I put my arms up, gesturing to the room and the stairs as I add, "Money's flowing. That's what counts."

"You're growing into what was already here—there's so much more to be done," he says, giving me the hard sell.

I made a deal with Jackson years back. Back when I was selling for Vito and he knew and he was in the academy. I'd keep things as they were. The cocaine, the pot, there's a demand for it from certain people in this town and the surrounding areas. I fill it, but keep it contained to just that.

Meth and heroin aren't an option. We both agree on that. It's how Jackson's mom died. I think it's the only reason the two of us work. He needs me keeping that shit out and I need him to keep the cops off our back.

Uptown, Fletcher makes a pretty penny from that shit. As does Mathews. As does Leroy.

They can sell, split and fight each other for it.

"Not interested at the moment," I answer Fletcher as I have for the past two years.

He lets out a low whistle, and I watch him watch Jameson land an uppercut against his opponent's jaw. The blood splatter only fuels the audience to scream for more. Even if it is an upset.

My eye catches sight of my men. Derrick and Liam are still surveying the room from the platform stage. Roman's in another corner, making another deal. Cade's got a grin from ear to ear as he's taking more bets.

"I like the system I've got going," I tell Fletcher, but I didn't need to give him that. He doesn't need or deserve an explanation. I wish I could pluck the statement from the air when he looks back at me. I'm taller than him, but it still feels like he's looking down at me.

"You're still learning," he says as he squares his shoulders and faces me. "There's more money to be made. You haven't even scratched the surface, my friend."

He puts his hand on my shoulder and I keep my expression firm. A moment passes, and anger swells inside of me. I won't repeat myself, and I won't humor him with more of this conversation.

"Are you good for the drop next week?" I ask bluntly and he drops his hand from my shoulder.

"Always open for your business," he tells me, and I offer him a tight smile, leaving him where he is and telling him to enjoy the show. He still urges me to "think about it" and I reassure him that if I'm in the market, I'll turn to him first.

The part that irritates me the most is that there's too much truth to Fletcher. The real money is in the harder shit. I'm the youngest leader of any crime organization for thousands of miles. And I do have a lot to learn. I picked up the pieces after a year of grappling for power. I took the deals I knew were already in place because we needed the money and the connections. Someone was going to take them, and I literally killed for it to be us.

Men like him, they aren't my friends. They don't need explanations. They'd get rid of me if they thought they could get away with it. I'm more than aware of that little fact.

"You look pissed," Derrick comments as I step up onto the stage to stand next to him.

The collar of my shirt feels tighter as I swallow down the rage. "What'd he say?" Derrick asks, referring to Fletcher.

"Everything's fine and set," I answer him and add, "Just pissed at myself."

"What happened?"

"I'm too fucking friendly," I tell him and the grin I give him makes him shake his head.

"Just your friendly neighborhood thug," he comments with humorous sarcasm.

"Something like that," I say and cross my arms, watching the fight and trying to hear the punches over the cheers.

"Did you decide what we're going to do about the potential problem?" I can feel Derrick's eyes on me, waiting for an answer to his question. I watch blood drip down Jameson's arm. I watch his jaw clench tighter as he lands blow after blow, the veins in his neck bulging.

Swallowing, I answer Derrick without looking at him. "There's no sign Mathews knows for sure."

"Right," he comments.

"All we can do is be ready if they come for us." Finally, turning to him I add, "And we can tie up the loose end."

"Loose end?" he questions but his gaze lights with the answer before I have to say it. "Wright."

"Wright," he repeats, although this time he breathes out long and heavy as he does.

"The sooner the better," I tell him.

"How do you want it done?" he asks, and I tell him I don't care.

A minute passes and the ref calls the fight, lifting Jameson's fist into the air. The man looks like he's barely standing on his own, like he needs that hand to be lifted just so he can stay upright. But he won.

"I thought you said Wright was with the cops?" Derrick's brow is lined with confusion. We don't fuck with the cops and they don't fuck with us.

"He is," I answer Derrick and lift a shoulder non-chalantly. "I'm tired of being friendly." I say the joke in a deadpan manner. "Kill Wright. From here on out we don't trust anyone to stay quiet."

Derrick huffs a laugh, although it's tight. "No more Mr. Nice Guy."

CHAPTER 12

Laura

THERE ARE NO STREETLIGHTS ON MY GRANDMA'S street. They're something the city never put in. So when I park, I don't turn off the car yet. I want that bit of illumination from my headlights as I take out my phone and peek at what Cami texted back.

I grin when I see her message about how she still hurts. But it's a good kind of hurt. I know the feeling. *Is every time like this*? she wrote in the last text.

Only the good ones, I reply before tossing the phone back into my purse. Taking a quick look around, I turn off the car and palm my keys. I've never liked the dark. But I especially don't like it here anymore.

I catch sight of a black sedan idling a few cars up. It would be hard to miss it. It's a sleek car and looks expensive; it looks like it doesn't belong here. The red brake lights come on and the car pulls away a little too fast, making their tires squeal. It's odd they'd drive away so quickly and because of that, I try to read the license plate, but all I get are the first two numbers. One and seven. I try not to care that I didn't see the rest of the plate. It's a habit I have, but this is just a random car.

It sends this weird vibe through me, though. Seeing that car take off... I can't shake it even though it's just a car. I don't know most of the people on this street anymore.

It's nothing, I tell myself and think about Cami's text again. But the odd feeling, that little stir of anxiousness, sits like a rock in the pit of my stomach.

All the good feelings from taking the practice entrance exam this morning seem to drain from me as I take the stone stairs up to the porch. I practically aced the test. I can't believe it. I didn't actually think I'd do well enough to even consider putting in my application anywhere. I never did well in school, so why would I? A hint of a smile tries to pull my lips up, but then I hear the gentle creak of the rusty porch swing. It lingers in the quiet air like the memories do. *Grandma would have been so proud.*

This place will always have memories around every corner and in every crevice, even if it's lifeless. Lacking everything it held when I was a kid. The dark and the quiet are reminders of everything that's gone. Everything that will never come back.

My eyes are on the ground while I walk, which is why I'm so shocked when I reach up to put the key in the door, only to find it already open.

The wooden frame is splintered. Confusion hits me first. I haven't even put the key in yet.

Thump.

The lock is still turned; I can see the hunk of metal as the door brushes open with the slight touch of my hand. Gasping, I try to stay calm, but I don't see how I can as the reality registers.

Thump.

The shoe print on the door is black against the white door. Someone kicked in the door.

"Fuck," I say and the curse leaves my lips in a whisper.

I'm half a step back, feeling the racing need to run take over when I smell smoke.

And then I see the bright red and orange flames beyond the cracked frame.

It's on fire. My grandma's house is on fire. No! God, no!

"Help!" I scream, gripping the keys so hard in my hand it feels like they've broken my skin.

My hands are shaking as I fumble in my purse. My keys drop harshly onto the concrete porch. Then something else, maybe my sunglasses; I don't know and I don't care.

I just need my phone.

I'm still shaking when I finally find it. Struggling with both hands to grip it and dial 9-1-1, I drop my purse and stand there on weak legs as I stare straight ahead, watching the bright red expand alongside billowing white and gray smoke. The hallway is clear, telling me it's the kitchen. The kitchen is on fire. The flames are high, almost to the ceiling. It's too far gone. *No, no, please tell me this is a nightmare.*

The operator is cool, calm and professional. Whatever he sounds like, I'm the opposite. Tears prick my eyes and my voice cracks as I tell him the address and that my house is on fire. Tell isn't the right word; maybe scream or cry would be better to describe it. My mind is a whirlwind, my lungs fail me and so does any form of common sense. He's asking me questions, asking if I'm safe and away from the fire.

He's going to tell me to step back. To get far away and keep my distance until help comes.

His voice comes through clear from the other end and I'm right.

I've never been one to just step back. Even with my blurred vision, I can see the fire is raging. But what if whoever broke in is still in there? What if I could find this bastard?

The phone drops in a swift motion, landing at my feet. A door slams open to my right, Mr. Timms's house, as I take a step into Grandma's.

"There's smoke from the back of your house!" Mr. Timms yells at me. I barely even hear him, although I recognize his ever-harsh tone. I sure as shit don't respond as I push open the door, feeling the wave of heat surround me instantly. I have to cover my mouth and nose with the crook of my arm.

The vise around my heart tightens as I walk quickly to the living room on the left. My coughing is involuntary as I pull open the coffee table drawer and take out a gun. The metal shines with the flick of flames as I get closer to the kitchen.

There's no chance whoever started this fire is still here. It's a raging storm of heat and flames at the back of the house. There's so much smoke; how long has it been going?

The sirens swarm from outside, but there's so much damage. Too much.

I can't even get to the bathroom, or the kitchen sink. My sobs are impossible to contain as I watch the destruction overwhelm this old house where I grew up.

A sound that resonates like the crack of a whip forces me to scream. Mr. Timms yells something from outside. He's closer now, yelling at me or the fire trucks. He sounds frantic but all I can hear is the sound of my home being burned to the ground as I watch.

I hear a crack, a snap and then a loud bang as the fire seems to grow along the wall like a vine. The pictures slam to the floor, leaving the shattered glass to skitter across the hardwood. I scream, covering my mouth as I stare in disbelief. A younger version of myself seated in my father's lap is slowly charred, lit aflame, and engulfed.

"The pictures," I say as my hands shake and I make a move to gather the ones closest to me and farthest away from the kitchen. Slipping the gun in the waistband at the back of my jeans, I feel the cold metal graze against my skin. With both hands up in the air, the smoke violates my lungs.

The first cough makes me heave in air, but the air is thick with soot and I collapse to the floor. I'm light-headed, taking in quick short pants, but I can breathe at least.

"Laura!" Seth's voice cuts through it all, like a bright light on the darkest of nights.

My neck cranes back to see him in the doorway. "Laura!" he screams louder as he runs into the house, his arm covering his face.

"Seth!" I scream as loud as I can and crawl to him, keeping my body low on the ground.

He breathes my name so softly when his eyes reach mine, I don't know how I heard it. Maybe it was the ghost of a memory filling in that actuality.

His movements are effortless as his arm wraps around my waist. I can hear my plea for the pictures at the back of my throat. I even reach for them, but Seth is strong, and the moment is hopeless. I'm so light-headed more than anything. It makes me weak.

I don't have a single picture of my father. I don't have any pictures of my grandmother.

They're all in this house.

The vision blurs in front of me as my skin feels cold and my head light. Outside is brighter than it's been this late. Everyone's porch light is on and everyone's watching. When my ass hits the hood of Seth's car, parked recklessly in Mr. Timms's front yard, I see how large the flames have gotten, how the house is completely engulfed. Maybe whoever did it had just been here.

I could have saved it all, if only I'd been here earlier.

Seth's hands are on me and he's talking, he's shaking me, but I can't stop crying. I can't stop this trembling.

I've never felt like it was all gone until this moment. It may have been empty, but it was still here. It held so much of me. Now what do I have?

My breathing is ragged as Seth pulls me into his hard chest. I feel him stroking my hair as I try to calm myself. Drying my eyes on his shirt, I watch as the hoses are pulled. I can smell the singe of burned wood as the flames rage against the downpour of water.

The firefighters are barking out orders nonstop. So much is going on that I can't focus; people talking, people looking at me, crowds gathered to watch my childhood home burning to nothing.

"Shhh," Seth soothes me. I close my eyes and listen to his heartbeat. I hear him shush me over everything else.

A paramedic is at our side too soon. I don't want to go; I don't want to leave, but Seth makes me.

I have to grab his wrist, holding it too tightly. "Someone broke in," I tell him, feeling my dry lips crack as I do. I stare into his dark eyes. They widen, a sense of recognition taking over. Carefully slipping my gun to him, hiding it under his jacket, I tell him before the medic returns to take me away, "Someone did this on purpose. Someone burned it all down." It's only when I'm in the ambulance with an oxygen mask over my face that I remember the black sedan. One and seven. I want to text Seth, but I don't have anything. Not my purse. Not my phone.

I refuse to forget. Someone might have seen whoever it was. Whoever it was may have taken everything from me. Whoever it was, is a dead man.

CHAPTER 13

Seth

M Y SKIN IS ICE COLD BUT EVERYTHING INSIDE
of me is on fire. A raging fire hotter and more
violent than the one at my back. I can feel the
heat, smell the burned wood, and it means nothing. The
chaos has everyone's full attention, but it means nothing
to me.

Someone did this.

They tried to hurt her. They tried to send a message.

Mathews is the only one I can think of. But why go
after Laura?

The heavy doors to the ambulance close one at a
time and the sound of them shutting, removing her from
my vision snaps my gaze to the EMT.

"You can't ride with her, but she'll be the top priority
in the emergency room. We already called it in."

You must be family. That's what the guy said to me
when they ripped her away.

There are only two things keeping me from chasing

down the ambulance and staying on its tail as they take her to the hospital.

The first is that Charlie said she's okay and that she'll be all right. It's just smoke inhalation they're concerned about. More importantly, he said he'll stay by her side until I'm there. I've known Charlie for years; he works with us on and off the clock. No one's getting near her room and Roman is already on his way to the hospital.

The second is that Jackson is in plain view when the ambulance leaves.

Dressed in his finest blues, his badge is on clear display and it reflects the light from behind us. It's waning as the water subdues the fire. I'll deal with Jackson first, and then I'm not leaving her side.

"Mr. King," he calls out and I huff in irritation. His footsteps are even and grow louder as he makes his way to me.

"Since when am I Mr. King to you?" I ask him when he stops in front of me, although my voice is lifeless, not hiding a damn thing I'm feeling.

The agony is something I didn't expect. It fucking hurts. The anger is better. Seeing her on a gurney in the back of an ambulance tears me up inside.

"I did this to her," I tell him, knowing exactly what I'm doing. I don't have many friends outside of my crew, but I need Jackson. I need all the help I can get.

Surprise colors his expression before he responds. He clears his throat and glances to his left and then right. "It was arson," he tells me as if I didn't know. A fire this large, this fast, there had to be an accelerant. Even if Laura hadn't told me, it doesn't take a genius to know.

"I figured as much," I tell him, looking coldly into his eyes at the thought of someone breaking into Laura's house.

"There were explosives too, Seth."

His lowered voice and this knowledge make my blood go cold. "They didn't go off. Duds I guess, but if they had, it would have blown up most of the block."

Leaning forward he asks, "You know who did it?"

I shake my head, trying to swallow the overwhelming feelings that make it hard to stand up right now as I say, "But I have suspects."

He tried to kill her. He tried to kill Laura. I can barely breathe.

Jackson's eyes read, *I told you so*, but he's a friend not to say it out loud and grind the heel of his shoe deeper into the pain and regret.

"I can't believe he'd go after a woman." *My woman.* "Fucking coward," I spit.

Breathing out, Jackson watches the fire behind me for a moment before telling me, "It's a good thing you got in there and dragged her out."

"Yeah," I answer him in a breath and turn to watch the blaze, but I can't do it. It almost took her away from me.

All I keep thinking as my muscles tighten to the point where I'm trembling is, *Mathews is a dead man. All of his men are dead. Anything he's ever touched, is dead.*

Rage is an adulteress. She comes at my weakest times, like now. Seeing the fire play on the metal of the police car, I imagine what I'll do to Mathews. It had to be him. He'll die a slow death. The rat, Wright? He can die slow too. Everyone who had a part. They will all suffer.

"Was she here when it happened?" Jackson asks with a careful tone, like what he's asking might make me snap. I shake my head no, remembering the little bits I've heard from Mr. Timms giving his statement as I held Laura.

"She came home and saw the fire, and ran in."

Jackson blows out a grunt. "Of course she did." His comment forces the faintest of laughs from me. *She's safe. She'll be all right. She's safe.* Just then I get a text from Roman. He's at the hospital now and ensuring Laura gets a private room.

Good. *Stay with her*, I tell him but he already knows.

"What are you going to do?" Jackson's question resonates with me. It's what I've done that's led to this.

"What do you think?" My answer is spoken darkly. He holds my gaze, taking it in with the seriousness it deserves. "If you have any insight to offer, now's the time," I prod when he doesn't respond.

"If I did, I'd tell you. Are you sure it's Mathews?" he asks me and a list of names runs through my mind, the many faces I've seen who hold nothing but contempt for me.

"No," I answer truthfully.

Jackson seems to consider something, but he only says, "If I hear anything, you'll be the first to know."

"I appreciate it."

He nods solemnly and stares past me. The night sky is darker than it was moments ago, and the streets are emptying out. Mr. Timms is seated on his porch, staring between the wreckage and me. My hard gaze doesn't deter him. The old man knows how this life works.

He knows this happened to her because of me. Everyone knows that.

"She's going to have to file a report," Jackson tells me and I nod in agreement.

"I'll tell her," I say although he looks anything but reassured.

"Do you have a statement to give?"

"No. I have to get to the hospital. To make sure she's okay," I tell him when I hear the sound of tires coming up behind us a little too fast. Both of our hands reach for guns, both of us on edge. Derrick's car screeches to a halt and Jackson and I both visibly relax when we see him get out and slam his door. It feels like war all over again, because that's what this is. An act of war.

"You do that." Jackson's already walking off, heading over to the fire truck when I call after him, "Thanks."

We may be on opposite sides of some things, but there's a loyalty between us that hasn't faded. Not yet. I imagine one day it will. All that will be left are the ashes of what used to be.

It seems like there's a lot of that going around.

"Yo." Derrick is at my side and out of breath before Jackson's even across the street. It's so dark now, I know he won't be able to see how bad it is. Not until morning.

"Is she okay?"

"We have to go to the hospital," I tell him and make my way to my car. My throat's tight and my jaw clenched as we walk past the last few onlookers.

"We see her, get her home, and then we have business to attend to." Feeling his eyes on me, I turn to look at him. A chill sweeps across my back, blowing the cold down my spine as I lower my voice. "We're killing Wright tonight, but first we need information. We need to know what he's been telling people and if this is Mathews's doing."

"Fuck." Derrick's response is accompanied by a mix between a groan and a snarl. With both hands running over his buzzed head he turns to look at Laura's old house. I watch it sink in. The disbelief, the outrage and then the guilt.

He swallows hard and looks down at the asphalt before looking back at me.

"We get her safe and then we settle this."

"Wright will be easy. If this is because of Mathews…" I trail off and shake my head, knowing that's a fight I'll need heavy backup for.

"We have Fletcher," he reminds me as I open my car door. "And cash to buy men who don't have a dog in this fight."

Looking between him and the rest of the scattered

crowd, I wonder how easy it's going to be to get to Mathews. To get revenge and ensure it doesn't happen again.

"I know we have men and the arms to do it," I finally respond and meet his gaze. "I just want it for myself. I want to kill this prick myself."

CHAPTER 14

Laura

SEVENTEEN. I KEEP THINKING ABOUT THE NUMBER and checking every plate that drives by the Club as I sit here in the front corner booth. I swear the worn amber leather smells like smoke. Everything smells like smoke still. Even after I washed up and put on clothes that had been tucked in drawers at Seth's house for a year now.

All I smell is smoke.

Another car rides by and it's not black, it's a dark red SUV, but I still check its plate. I've been doing this all day. I don't need to find its owner though, not if what Derrick said in the hospital is true. Still, I watch, I check. I'm on guard and trapped here in this booth.

Seth doesn't want me to leave the Club; I think he's having Roman keep an eye on me.

I'll be better when they find that car. I remember that feeling I had. Why didn't I listen to it? Gut instincts happen for a reason. That air of danger was meant to warn me. I know it deep down. And yet, I couldn't even remember more than two numbers. It's okay though, if what Derrick said is right.

Cami's voice jostles me from my thoughts about last night. "Hey, you good?"

"Yeah," I answer her as quickly as I can. I have to clear my throat and take a drink of the Sprite she set down in front of me.

"Ugh," I groan and nearly spit it out, not expecting the strong taste of vodka. With the back of my hand over my mouth, I barely keep it down.

"I thought you liked vodka?"

"You spiked it?"

"You need a drink," she says, emphasizing the word *need* before sitting down next to me. The seat groans and I watch another car go by. It's black this time, but another SUV and not a sedan. Still, my heart starts to race, pounding against my rib cage. I want them to find whoever it was so I can stop worrying that he'll come back. That's what it comes down to. I fucking hate this feeling that claws at me.

"I know you're shaken up," Cami says, trying to soothe me. She has no idea. I have no intention of telling her that it wasn't an accident. She doesn't need that worry in her life. But I wish I had my friend to confide in.

As she consoles me, telling me the insurance company will pay out and how she's certain some things will be able to be recovered from the house, I wonder if this is what Seth feels like when I try to talk to him after a hard day. Her hand lands on my knee under the table and she looks at me with wide, innocent eyes. "It's going to be okay," she tells me like she means it. Like she knows for sure it will.

I've heard it so many times. *It's going to be okay*. It never is.

"I hope so," I answer her weakly.

She pats my knee, giving me a sweet smile.

"You *know* it will," she says with a raised brow, and a look on her face that says, *we're choosing to be positive.*

In this moment, I almost want to tell her the truth just so I can see that look fall.

I want to tell her how I told Seth about the black sedan and how Derrick knew right away who it belonged to, or at least he thinks he does. I want to tell her all this shit happened because of the men we love. Dumb for dick. It's a saying Cami has when certain women come into this bar. We are dumb for dick.

That would take that smile right off Cami's face and wake her up about who she's dating.

All the snide thoughts ping-pong around my head and I know they're only there because I bit my tongue when Seth leaned down to kiss me before he left. I didn't have the words to give him last night. I felt it all bottled up, but nothing would come. This morning though, I'm full of plenty of words. They aren't meant for Cami though.

"Right," I tell her, forcing a smile to my face. "I know everything will be okay," I lie to her.

She grabs the edge of the open textbook on the table, dragging it to face her so she can read it.

"I'm not sure you're going to get much enjoyment from *Physiological Integrity* by—" I say as I grab the book so I can lift it up and peek at the spine of the textbook.

"I don't even know how to pronounce the first word," Cami says, cutting me off and then she laughs. It's contagious so I end up laughing too, for the first time today. She glances at the papers in front of me.

"Applications," I say, answering her unspoken question. "I got a really good score on that practice test I took so I'm applying. I'm really going to do it. I think I have a good shot at getting into a lot of good schools."

"Oh." Just like that, her happiness vanishes. "Where are you going?" she asks and her hands find her lap. She picks at her thumbnail—a nervous habit she's had for as long as I've known her.

"Not far," I reassure her.

"Right," she says and nods her head with her eyes closed and that simper reappears. "Seth wouldn't want you to go very far." With her worries eased, I add another to mine.

The school I want to attend, one I thought I'd never be able to get into, is across the country. *Maybe I could just leave for a little while.* The voice in my head is small and hesitant. *Just a little while, just to get some distance.*

"Hey." Cami's voice brings me back to the moment. "It's going to be all right," she says, encouraging me.

"I know," I answer her and snag my pen as if I'm

going to fill out these applications. I've been staring at them all day and I can't bring myself to do it. I lie to her again, but it feels easier this time because I picture Seth telling me the same, like he has so many times, "It'll be all right."

◎

I've never thought of myself as strong. Never.

I grew up surrounded by men with guns. Men who made threats and made jokes about women who looked like me. Jokes about how easy women were. My father would tell me that all men were pigs but him.

He was a pig too, though.

I suppose it didn't bother me that I wasn't a strong woman until tonight. Until I'm here sitting cross-legged on the floor of Seth's living room, sunk into the deep blue rug I picked out for him, staring at cardboard boxes filled with my few remaining possessions that weren't destroyed by the fire or the water damage.

"We can get the smell out," Seth tells me from the kitchen. I listen to him open the fridge and get a beer. It's followed by the sound of a drink being poured and I figure that one's for me.

The words I've been thinking all day are stuck somewhere deep down my throat. Like I've swallowed them, even though inside I'm begging for them to come up. He needs to hear exactly what I'm thinking.

He needs to know.

I have to stare at the large black imprint on the cardboard box to say it. It comes out all wonky, like it's scratched its way up. "I want you to get out of the business."

"What?" I hear him reply from the kitchen and close my eyes. I feel lighter already having gotten that off my chest. Even if I know exactly how he'll respond.

"You need to get out." My voice is louder this time, stronger, and for a moment I question if I was really so weak. Until I see him.

Seth makes me weak.

"Get out?" he questions but it doesn't sound like it. His expression is emotionless at best, and disapproval riddles his gaze.

He hands me the drink he made. Smells like Sprite, and I imagine there's vodka swirling in it alongside the ice cubes. He knows it's my favorite, which makes this conversation hurt all the more.

I can't say it again, not while he's looking at me like that. It feels like my chest is hollowed out. Like my own damn heart abandoned me. My throat's dry when I try to explain, but still nothing comes. Yeah, I was never a strong woman.

"You want me to get out of the life," he says, repeating my words back to me with no emotion behind them and then stares straight ahead, still standing while I'm seated. His gaze is on the blank TV screen that's hanging on the wall when he takes a drink of his beer. "It's not like that, Babygirl."

"Then what is it like?" I ask him, listening to the ice clink against the glass and taking a heavy gulp and then another. There isn't enough alcohol on the West Coast to save me from this moment.

Seth's quiet and so I lift my gaze to his. "Because I don't like the way it feels anymore. I don't think—"

"You knew," he says, cutting me off, and his tone is accusatory. It's what he always goes to. I knew he was in the life when I started seeing him. I did. I admit that. Times were different then. It was kill or be killed. There was no in-between. I fell in love; how could I not? I'm not the strong one. I was never the strong one.

The bottom of his beer clinks down hard on the coffee table. The cords in his neck tighten as he swallows and looks down at me. He opens his mouth, but he doesn't have any more words for me.

It hurts so fucking much. "I love you," are the only words I can whisper. That's what it always comes down to for me.

And so it's a stalemate, but I can't face a stalemate anymore. I'll take the hit. I'm terrified, but I'm trying to be strong.

Dropping down to his knees, he cups my jaw in his hand. I don't even realize my bottom lip is trembling until his thumb is there, running over it, caressing me and gentling the pain that keeps me from looking into his eyes.

"I'm sorry," I whisper and he whispers back, "Don't be. There's nothing to be sorry about."

He doesn't get it. He doesn't understand and I can't say it.

It's this life or me.

I can't say it because it's wrong. I can't. I can't do it.

The first kiss is gentle, caressing. I'm eager for it, but when he deepens it, I pull back, covering my hunger for him with my hand over my mouth. Bracing myself on my left hand, I lean backward and dare to meet his gaze.

A raw desire, coupled with a primitive agony, stares back at me. I swear I must have known this man in another life. He was made for me and I for him, but I don't want this life.

"I can't live like this." I don't know how I manage to speak, each word dangling there between us like easily broken threads. "I want you to get out of it," I repeat. "I need you to."

Seth takes a moment, watching me, considering my words before standing up and turning his back to me.

He's silent as he heads to the kitchen and I continue watching him from where I am. I watch him finish the beer and then grab his keys from the blue bowl.

"Don't go," I say. The next words rush out of me. "I need you." How selfish I feel in this moment is almost unbearable. Especially when he turns to look at me again.

He raises the hand holding the keys in the air, to point at me. "And I need you," he says like it's a confession that will bury him.

"Don't leave, Seth. Please, we can talk this out."

A smile akin to a sick joke graces his face but it quickly disappears. "There isn't much talking that can change our situation, Babygirl."

Hopelessness is all I can hear in his tone. He can't be the hopeless one. I cover my face with both hands, feeling an onslaught of emotions. Tears prick but I don't let them come.

Be strong, Babygirl. I hear Seth's voice in my head. Even at my lowest moments, the memory of him is there. It will kill me to lose him. It will kill me to stay.

My shoulders are shaking as I rock myself. I've never felt like this. This misery that feels so much worse than mourning. It's worse because I have control over it. I can make it stop. I can just say the right words. I can pretend it's okay. I can stay here with him and pretend I don't feel this ominous sense of dread. That I'm not constantly scared for not just me but him too.

The keys slam down on the counter and within a split second, Seth's strong chest is pressed to my back. His arms are around me. He rocks me until I've stopped. It's easy to calm down when he's here. His smell, his voice. The way he loves me even if he doesn't say it.

I have nothing without him. I have absolutely nothing. I cling to him.

"It's okay," he tells me and even with all the misery I want to believe him.

"I have nothing left," I finally speak.

"I need you to leave because I'm terrified," I confess to him. "Bad things happen here. I don't have control over any of it." My words make him pull back, breaking his hold on me.

He doesn't say anything for a long time. I grab the cocktail he made me and practically chug it. It does nothing. There is no relief from this whatsoever.

"You need time—"

"No," I say, shaking my head and cutting him off before he's finished.

"You need time for me to show you it's okay. You need time because it's been a rough few years."

"It can get rougher," I speak without thinking. It's the truth though, and the look in his eyes tells me he knows. He's all too aware. I rest my cheek on the sofa, thinking maybe I've been like Cami all the time we've been together, and I've just now crossed to the other side.

I'm not strong enough for this side of things. I wish I were, but I'm nothing compared to him. He should know that. It's easy to see.

"Hey, come here," he says and his voice is gentle. He's always soft with me. This strong man with rough edges and a past that would frighten most… his tone caresses me. I can't help it. I'm drawn to him like a moth to a flame.

I crawl over to him, settling down in his lap. He's so tall and his shoulders are so much wider than me that it feels perfect here. He's warm, and when I lay my cheek against his shoulder, peeking up at him and wondering why he picked me, he kisses me. Stopping my questioning, stopping the pain. It's all replaced by an immediate spike of heat. An immediate desire.

Does he feel it too? How it soothes every inch of me. How that lust turns to wildfire in my blood and nothing stands a chance in its path. With his fingers at my chin, he keeps me still while he breaks the kiss. When I open my eyes, feeling the forgotten beads of moisture in my lashes, he's there, staring at me. His light blue eyes shine with devotion. It's real. I know it's real.

His cadence is rough when he says, "Let me make you feel better."

"We have to talk about this," I tell him as if it's a demand, but I'm begging him. "I lost everything."

"I'm sorry," he says, rushing the words out. "I will make it up to you, but you can't leave and neither can I." The resolution in his tone forces me to bury my face in the crook of his neck. I know I won't be okay either way.

His whisper, his touch, and the air around us are all I have to stay whole. "Let me make you feel better."

CHAPTER 15

Seth

WHAT ABOUT THE CHAIR IN THE LIVING *room?* I text Derrick and wait. All I can hear is the sound my foot was making earlier. The tapping on the leg of the steel chair as I stared at Wright's body.

Four hours of digging for information with Connor's blade, and he swore he didn't tell Mathews. He screamed it, he begged for us to believe him. But I didn't. Hours later, at home in the kitchen, my foot's motionless but the anxiousness is still there.

The black sedan doesn't belong to one of Mathews's men, it belongs to one of Fletcher's.

I don't want to believe it. More than that, I still don't believe Wright, not even his dying words.

I don't know. It's in rough shape. It takes me a moment to remember what Derrick's talking about. Right, the wreckage from the fire.

Try to save it, I text back and inhale as deeply as I

can. I can't even salvage a fucking chair, let alone this fucked-up situation.

If Wright didn't tell Mathews, and it was Fletcher...

Are you ready?

Ready to find out if Fletcher double-crossed me. *Yeah*, I message him, *I'm ready.*

How is she? he messages before I've even set my phone down. The whole crew knows; they all know someone wanted Laura dead.

We assumed it was Mathews, but thinking it might be Fletcher... fuck, that means we have no one to back us up. Leroy won't go after Fletcher. We can't trust Mathews.

Derrick's the only one who knows we're not okay. I lean forward on the counter, my forearm brushing the beer, which is now warm and still full. I can't move from this spot. I can't do it.

She was trying to leave me last night. She's never done that before.

I could see it in her eyes that I'm losing her, so I lie to him, *I can keep her; she's just going through shit right now.*

To my right, I picture her there, sitting on the rug and looking up at me with goodbye in her eyes and I lose it. Tears pricking at the back of my eyes, I slam my fist down on the counter.

She loves you.

Derrick's message means so little. She does love me, and I thought I could keep her forever because of it. But love isn't that easy. It's not that strong either.

I lay with her in bed until she fell asleep, and then

I took out all that pain and rage on Wright. He didn't feel enough of it though. Even with his dying breath, he didn't feel loss like I was feeling.

Maybe Fletcher's henchman will feel it. Luke Hartley. The owner of the black Audi with license plate number 175632. The fucker who took off. Something tells me I'm not going to believe him either. It'll be more than four hours though. It's going to take more than four hours to make him feel this pain that's inside of me right now.

Leroy's guy said 220.

Derrick's text forces me to move to the bedroom. Every step is careful and quiet and I don't look to my right as I pass the living room. I swear the ghost of last night is there, watching me.

Two hundred and twenty thousand for him to send up four men in case we need them to go after Fletcher. The code to the safe is our anniversary date. It's three days and one year after the shit at Hammers went down. It took me that long to get her to love me enough to give in.

I only get the first two numbers punched in before I rest my forehead on the safe, feeling the cool metal against my hot skin.

Derrick texts something else, probably asking if he should tell Leroy's guy it's a go or not. I have to enter in the rest of the code and check the tally inside. There's a pad of paper I use to track it all.

It'll be close and it'll slow down business, but we can manage.

I text him confirming it's a go, and that I'm on my way before slamming the safe door shut and getting out of this house as fast as I can.

When I start the car, I sit there for a moment, staring at the damn house I had built in the middle of nowhere to protect us. She would have been safe here. If she'd listened to me. I need to remember to tell her that. I can convince her.

If she'd listened and moved in with me by now, she'd have been safe. I should have made her move in. I should have told her she needed to let go sooner.

Fuck, it's my fault. It's all my fault.

A series of pings comes through on my phone, and I have to calm myself down, shaking off this regret, this feeling like I'm losing her to read what Derrick's telling me.

They've got Luke, but more importantly, Fletcher's warehouse was broken into, their stash stolen.

Mathews? I question him. Mathews went after Fletcher? Mathews thinks Fletcher is the one who screwed him over.

Derrick's reply back sends a chill down my spine.

I don't know, but Fletcher thinks it was us.

CHAPTER 16

Laura

D R. JUNE'S BEEN OFF DURING THE PROCEDURES. I've been here for at least two hours, subjected to stress tests and being poked and prodded.

No black dress and heels today for the doctor. She's wearing the sneakers I'd wear as a nurse, which I find ironic.

"Everything okay?" I ask her as she looks at my chart. She entered the room at least a minute ago and didn't even say anything to me. She's just looking at the results of all the tests.

"Fine," she says then gives me a tight smile and returns to the clipboard.

I don't really feel fine. There's nothing that's fine. The way she's been makes me think something is very, very wrong.

In most cases, medication is all that's required to manage arrhythmia. But then there are the more severe cases.

I channel my inner Cami, wishing she were here. We're

going to be positive, I tell myself. Dr. June just got dumped is all. Yeah, that makes me feel better. *When did I get this bitter?*

"You didn't bring anyone?"

I stare back at Dr. June when she sighs heavily and lowers the clipboard to the metal cart to her right.

"Forgot to ask," I lie to her. She doesn't need to know that Cami stood me up. That little tidbit makes me feel a little more lonely. I've realized I don't like being lonely.

"I'm going to prescribe you a medication," Dr. June tells me before pulling out a pad of paper from the back of the clipboard. I watch as she scribbles out a prescription. "You can have it filled at any pharmacy. Make sure you take it daily," she drones on, like she's reading from a script.

I interrupt her telling me about possible side effects to ask, "So everything's fine?"

"Well, you have an irregular heartbeat, but it's treatable with a calcium blocker. Your heart itself is in good condition, which is a great sign. The arrhythmia is virtually harmless, but this medicine will do the trick to keep it beating normally."

"Medicine to keep your heart beating normally," I echo and I can't help it when my eyes water.

"Yeah." The doctor finally shows some emotion as she says, "We should all have access to it, shouldn't we?" Her sad joke mirrors the look of despair I've been feeling from her for the past two hours.

"That's a joke." She quickly corrects herself and gathers the clipboard as she stands. As if I didn't get it.

"I know," I tell her solemnly. I'm such a weirdo, I want to stand up and hug this woman. A woman I know nothing about. A woman I've been inwardly bitter toward. Am I really that lonely?

"This is for you." Handing me the script, she tells me how I can exit the office once I've changed out of my patient gown. She's back to her robotic self with a fake smile as her parting gift.

I accept it and tell her I hope she has a great day. Everyone says that, but I do mean it. I hope she can at least feel that I mean it.

When she's gone, I sit back on the crinkled paper and stare at the prescription before getting dressed. Pills to keep my heart going. I'm going to really need these.

Checking my phone, I see Cami hasn't answered. It's so not like her. She told me she'd come. Regardless, I let her know that I'm all right. I haven't told her about last night yet. Maybe she already knows, maybe Seth told Derrick and Derrick told her.

My face crumples as I lean forward, as does the fucking paper under my ass. It mocks me, and oddly enough, I'm fine with it.

I deserve to be mocked. How did I really think this was going to end?

I text Cami again, telling her I really need her and that I have to tell her something. All the while I get dressed, I watch my phone, waiting for the buzz or for it light up. Anything.

But I get nothing.

Even as I'm driving, I expect her to say something. I convince myself her phone is broken and when I do that, I feel slightly better. Nothing compared to the relief I feel when I see her car in Seth's driveway.

Oh thank God, I think and breathe out in relief. She's been waiting for me to get back. I knew it, I knew her phone was just broken or something.

I haven't parked a car this fast in a long damn time. Gathering my purse, I climb out and prepare to tell her everything. She needs wine for this and I need vodka.

Maybe we should go out first and get enough booze to last us through this.

Even as I'm coming up to the door, I think I already know what she's going to tell me and it calms the deepest part of me.

You love him. I can hear her voice over the sound of the keys. She locked the door. Of course she did, she's in there all alone. I have to fiddle with the lock to get the door open, and through the clang of metal, I hear her tell me that I love him and that love will find a way.

She's told me before. *So long as you choose love, it will all work out.*

Breathing out at the door, rocking the key out of the lock, I let her unspoken words sink in. She's right. I just need her to remind me. And I need Seth because I love him.

It will all be okay.

I center myself for the first time since the fire two nights ago. I have to laugh a little as I push open the door and speak loud enough for her to hear me in the living room. "I didn't even need the pep talk; you've given me so many, I can hear your voice in my head."

My smile fades when I don't see her in the living room. She's not in her usual spot. We each have a spot.

I turn on the light in the hallway, and even though the light's off in the bathroom, I still check for her there. "Cami?" I call out, and she doesn't answer.

That gut feeling, that instinct of danger I felt two nights ago? It's back. It's chilling. "Cami?" I call out louder as I head for my bedroom door.

Why would she be in there? *Maybe she had to sleep. She's only sleeping*, I lie to myself. I know it's a lie. I'm so aware of it before I hear the creak of the bedroom door opening.

Sobs hit me hard and fast as I fall to the floor on my knees.

"Cami," I whisper her name and reach toward her. "No, Cami."

She's so cold. She's so cold.

Years ago

Everyone in this cafeteria is somehow both staring at me and not looking at me at all. Everyone except Seth and his friends. They're two tables over, sitting at the one closest to the doors, and when I look up they don't mind that my eyes catch theirs every once in a while, but everyone else immediately looks away.

They all know what happened two weeks ago and what happened this past weekend. Shit, the bruise on my cheek is still there although it's an ugly green and I can't stop crying every ten minutes. Just as I'm reaching up to touch the bruise, as if I'll be able to tell if the makeup is still covering it or not, Cami sits next to me.

Our table is empty except for the two of us, so when her tray hits the table and she climbs into the cheap benches our high school bought, the whole thing jostles.

I imagine I'm looking at her just like everyone else is looking at me. Slack-jawed. None of my so-called friends sit by me anymore. She did though.

"I'm sorry I wasn't here after the accident," she tells me as she cracks open a soda. "Are you doing okay?"

I'm still staring at her when she turns in her seat, tucking her right foot under her and then squares her shoulders. "I feel like a shit friend; I just found out on the way down here."

I don't say anything. She's talking about my dad and the accident. I don't want to cry. Not when everyone has such a good view of the spectacle I am.

"You want to get out of here? You want to yell? You want to cry?"

"No," I finally answer her and stare down at my tray. There's only an apple and a cold slice of pizza. I don't want to eat. Everything has changed and nothing's all right.

"What can I do?" Cami asks me and it's the first time anyone's asked me that. Seth tells me what to do, he has

for over two weeks now and I appreciate it some moments, but I need time to myself, time to process.

Other than him and his crew, no one else asks me anything. They don't talk to me. It's like they're suddenly afraid of me.

Cami reaches her arms around me. It takes me a moment to realize she's hugging me. That's the moment I realize how big her boobs are and the thought actually makes me laugh a little on the inside.

"What the hell is wrong with me?"

I don't realize I've said it out loud until Cami shakes her head, her long blonde hair swishing around her shoulders. "Not a damn thing," she tells me and spears her fork through a grape. She eats them all like that, with a fork.

It's quiet for a moment, but Cami keeps trying to make small talk, keeps hinting at asking whether I need something or if I'm all right. She asks me if she should just shut up and I tell her no.

"Whatever you do, please don't stop talking. I need to talk about something."

"Anything?" she asks and her gaze drifts to the crew of guys we were both once afraid of.

"Almost anything," I correct her and a hint of a smile graces her lips. Again, this sad laugh comes over me, but this time the sound is heard.

"You're going to be okay," she tells me. "I love you."

It's the first time she's told me that. Everything about her makes me think I've found my friend soul mate.

"I'm happy you're here," I tell her with sincerity and then smile and say "I love you" back.

I have a moment to sniffle and get a grip while she takes a large bite of her pizza.

"You ever wish you could just pick up and leave?" I ask her. It's all I've been thinking about for the last three days. I can't though. Grandma needs me now more than ever.

Cami eyes one of Seth's friends, I think his name is Derrick. Then she licks a bit of sauce from her lip and tells me yeah, she has. "Everyone wishes they could leave and start over sometimes."

There's so much comfort in what she says. "Where would you go?" she asks and then takes a bite. She covers her mouth, still chewing when she tells me enthusiastically, "I know where I'd go."

"Where?" I question her and she finishes her bite and washes it down with her drink before telling me with the widest smile, "I'd love to go to Paris."

"The city of love," I breathe out and pick up my apple. As I'm taking a bite, she tells me how her uncle went and brought back a pop-up picture book for her when she was a kid. "It's my favorite; I still have it. Paris Up, Up and Away."

"When you go—"

"I'm taking you with me," she declares, cutting me off then continues eating, like I should have known better. I should have known we'd go together.

"I'd love to go to Paris," I tell her weakly before the tears fall again and this time I don't know why. I was doing so good.

Cami holds me tight and when she sees someone staring, she tells them to fuck off.

We never went to Paris. She has to go to Paris.

"Cami, you have to wake up. Cami, wake up."

CHAPTER 17

Seth

"THE CAR WAS PARKED OUT FRONT," DERRICK explains as I drag the metal chair across the concrete floor. The basement of Club Allure has seen more blood in the last two nights than I ever intended. We make do with what we have though.

"It was him. He's saying something different though," Connor informs me as I sit across from Mr. Hartley.

I let my head loll to the right as I take in the knots at his wrist. "He's been fighting it, looks like." The coarse rope has left dark pink marks around his wrist. There's a hint of blood on the loose threads too.

"Had to tie his chest to the chair too. Wrists and ankles weren't doing it," Connor tells me, his gaze steady on our unwelcome guest. The rope is wrapped twice across his chest. "He kept falling over."

"Is that what caused the gash on his head? Or did you two start the party without me?"

Roman's out front, keeping an eye out. The four of

us, Derrick, Connor, this Luke fuck, and myself, are the only people within four miles of Linel Centers.

"Seth," Derrick says then scoots his chair forward and I glance at him but I have to do a double take. The way his forehead is creased, his lips pressed in a firm line and his eyes reflecting doubt... I don't like it. I don't like it at all.

Connor steps forward, ripping the rag out of Luke's mouth. Luke's body heaves forward as he sucks in air in between coughs.

I share a look with Derrick then one with Connor, both of them chilling me to the bone. Derrick nods his head at the man in the chair, whose gaze is focused on the floor. "Listen," he mouths to me. My muscles ache to let out the rage. It takes everything I have just to stay in my seat.

"You'll never get away with it," Luke says, threatening us the moment he's able to speak. His cadence is rough and from the split lip and gash in his head, I can guarantee he's hurting.

"The threats always come first," I tell Luke, speaking lowly, but I sit back in my chair, listening to the ranting man.

I crack my knuckles one by one, waiting.

Luke's head raises slowly and his brown eyes find mine, the hate firmly in place. "First the warehouse, then me? Fletcher will never let you get away with it."

"We didn't hit the warehouse."

"I didn't hurt Laura," Luke spits out immediately

after my admission. He said her name. I can't sit here and listen to this man say her name and get away with it. The steel chair I'm sitting on is practically nothing, flying backward as I lunge forward. The skin on my knuckles stretches tight and nearly splits as I land a blow on Luke's jaw, screaming at him, "You don't get to say her name."

His chair falls backward, the steel clanging against the cement as I tower over him, heaving in air.

Connor's behind me in a split second, his hands on my biceps, pulling me back. He doesn't have to pull hard; I wasn't going to beat the shit out of him.

"He can't say her name," I explain to Connor, who looks up at me bewildered. It takes a hard look from me before he corrects himself.

Groaning on the ground, Luke spits up blood, and then looks me in the eyes as he says, "I would never go after a woman. Fletcher..." He has to pause and spit and when he does, I can already see the bruise forming from his lower jaw up to his high cheekbone. "Fletcher wouldn't go after the women. He'd never do that, and you fucking know it."

He's out of breath by the time he adds *bastards* to the end of his statement. Derrick eyes me all the while he hauls Luke and his chair back upright to a sitting position.

I lower myself in front of Luke, crouching so he's at eye level. "Then why was your car there?"

I expect him to deny it. To call my girl a liar, which

will earn him a matching bruise on the other side of his pretty boy face. He doesn't though.

"It was stolen," he tells me. For a moment, doubt sets in. Everything that was hot, turns cold. I don't let a damn thing show on my expression though.

"When we found him, he was in the car," Derrick tells me quickly.

"Fletcher would kill me if I fucked with you. He said we needed you and then this shit happened."

Grabbing the back of his chair, I pull Luke closer to me, listening to the metal scrape against the floor as I do. My face is inches from his when I ask him, "Who stole your car?"

A faint smile wobbles on his lips and the bastard starts to cry. "You won't believe me."

"Who stole your car?" I scream the question in his face, feeling the rage tear its way up my throat.

Luke lets out a sick laugh and looks away to tell me, "I don't know."

Cursing, I step back, shoving Luke's chair when I do although he doesn't topple over. I believe him. And that's a big fucking problem.

Doubt and insecurity crawl their way up my spine.

"You better think of something," Connor tells the henchman. "I don't think my boss is too happy about the current situation."

"I thought it was a stupid fucking kid who'd figured out it was mine and got wise."

"Care to elaborate?" Derrick asks. I keep my back to

Luke all the while, listening, trying to piece everything together.

"Someone stole it while I was collecting dues. I was pissed."

"You file a police report?" Connor asks with a smirk on his face. He's fucking with him. Men like us don't call the cops. Luke sneers at him.

"Boss," Derrick interrupts me when my phone starts vibrating against the metal. It's still sitting on the steel chair. Turning from where I stand, I wait for him to tell me who it is. "Fletcher."

I shake my head no, and Derrick drops the phone. The vibrations get louder.

"How did you get it back?" I question Luke.

"I didn't. Whoever it was, parked it on Fifth and Rodney. I figured they learned it was my car and what I'd do to them. They didn't touch it. Not a scratch."

Luke's expression looks hopeful although his eyes are a well of despair.

"Call him back, put him on speaker." I give the command to Derrick. "If you want to live, you'll be quiet until I tell you to speak."

"Do you believe me? You have to believe me."

"I don't trust anyone anymore," I answer him. That bit of hope he has falls. I see it, I recognize it. "I mean what I say. Don't speak until I call for you."

"Don't have to call his boss," Derrick says. The second he lifts the phone, it's vibrating again. I watch him tap the screen and then nod.

"Fletcher." I answer the call on speaker and Fletcher's voice is quiet on the other end, but it still fills the large empty room.

"King." It's quiet as I listen to my heart pound. "It seems there are some misunderstandings."

"Is that what we're calling it?" I ask Fletcher and I can hear him huff into his phone. Short and humorless.

"I don't believe it was you," Fletcher tells me and my gaze lifts to Derrick's. I can see Luke in my periphery, looking between the three of us. He's tense, and I'm sure he's aware that his life depends on this call.

"We took your man," I say, speaking clearly. I need him to know, to show him my cards.

"Because you believed it was me," he surmises.

"I believed it was him," I answer honestly.

"Because she told you—"

"She stays out of it," I say, cutting him off. For the first time, anger slips into the conversation and I stare at Luke, who's eager to scream out, but he's silent. "She stays out of it," I repeat. Calmer, with more control.

The air is tense and hot. It suffocates me.

"She stays out of it," Fletcher agrees. "Someone is playing us, King, and I don't like it. I don't care for the fact that you played into their hand."

"It has to be Mathews," I speak and close my eyes, trusting my gut. Gut instincts get you everywhere in this life.

"He stole my stash the way you stole his. He stole my right-hand man's car to set me up. He played us, pitting us against one another.

"He's done it before," Fletcher continues. "It's how he's able to grow as fast as he does. Everyone who doesn't deal with him finds themselves at war with someone else."

He's waiting on a response from me, but all I can think is how much I've fucked up. How bad this shit has gotten. Everything is fucked.

"Did you kill him?" Fletcher asks when I don't say a damn word. I tilt my head toward Luke, giving him the permission he's been dying for.

"I'm here, Boss," Luke tells him. His eyes dart between all of us as if he expects us to kill him as he's speaking to Fletcher. I stand still, not knowing what will happen next.

It's a cardinal sin to break trust in this way of life. It's paper thin to begin with and I shot a cannon through it.

"What would you have done?" I ask, knowing where I stand. He thought it was us. His first instinct when his warehouse was robbed, was that it was us. I'm not the only one who made that judgment, but I'm the one who acted first.

All I can hear is the heavy breathing to my left from Luke, whose wild eyes tell me he thinks he's done for. Fletcher takes his time answering.

"I can't answer that," he finally speaks and his answer pisses me off.

Stepping closer to the phone, and feeling the anger write itself on my face, I question him, "And why is that?"

Derrick watches me closely. I can feel his eyes boring into me, but he doesn't say a damn word.

"Because I don't love anyone," he answers. "I have no wife; I have no kids. You love Laura."

I can hear Derrick swallow, and then his hand is on my shoulder. We fucked up. We never should have touched Luke.

"I can make you a promise right now that before I question your men, if that time were to ever arise, I'll speak to you first."

"That's all I can do."

"It would be wise to let her go. You're good at what you do, but not when it comes to her."

"Untie him," I tell Connor in a murmur and instead of engaging Fletcher and his romantic advice, I move the conversation to what matters. "Mathews needs to pay for this."

"We need more men," he says and Fletcher's voice is easier now, closer to the way it was just the other night.

"We have them; I have the money. I've got the cash to give to the crews down south."

"I want to be clear that I am loyal to you, King. But if you do something this stupid again, I will kill you."

"I hear your threat loud and clear." I did what I had to do. I did what any man would have done. If he tries to kill me, I'll happily kill him first. There is no love lost between Fletcher and me. I will use him, and he will use me. That's all this is. We trust that the other is needed, and when that need no longer exists, one of us will kill the other. I can already see it playing out before my eyes.

"It's a promise, not a threat."

"Boss," Luke speaks up as the rage rings in my blood. "His address." Luke pushes out the words as if they'll stop a bomb from going off.

"Fuck," Fletcher hisses into the phone. "Mathews had his car."

My stomach churns and I don't know why.

"And?" I question.

"I had to check you out. You can't be pissed." His preface to this confession sits uneasily in the pit of my gut. "We're still cool and that's how we're going to stay," he states firmly.

"What did you do?" I ask and the contempt is clear in my voice.

"If someone from Mathews's crew was in my car, he could have your home address."

The room tilts and spins. "Laura," I breathe.

I end the call instantly, texting her not to go home, but she's already messaged me. She said I have to come home. That was an hour ago.

CHAPTER 18

Laura

I T WAS SUPPOSED TO BE ME. IT SHOULD HAVE BEEN ME.
The thoughts don't stop as I rock on the floor, staring at Cami. With a trembling bottom lip, I try to say her name again, but my throat is raw.

At first I thought I should run, in case whoever had been here was waiting for me. I can't leave Cami though. I can't leave her. Not like this.

I want to touch her, but instead I shove my hands into my lap. Her skin is already cold. She's been dead for hours now. I bet she came to drive me. She liked to do that, surprise me with coffee that's probably sitting in her car this very second.

She came to be a friend, and it got her killed. I got her killed. I'll never be able to forgive myself.

The carpet is harsh on my legs as I crawl backward, trying to keep myself from returning to her side. Every few minutes I think it's not real. She's not actually dead. I'm wrong, I'm seeing things, this is all a bad joke.

And then I touch her, I cry out her name. I shook her once and the clots on her throat gave way, letting a small trickle run down to her shoulders and onto my hand.

Her blood. Cami's blood.

She's really dead.

My hands are shaking. Even when I grip them together as tight as I can, feeling the blood rushing inside of them, they don't stop shaking.

I should have been the one who was here. It should be me who was tied up. The gouges around her wrists are so deep. Like they used wire to do it.

I can't stop staring at her. Every inch of her. Every bit of evidence showing what they did to her.

And I know damn well it was supposed to be me.

The taste of salt from my tears is overwhelming, as is the heat on my face. Everything is hot and I can barely breathe; I'm suffocating, waiting in the bedroom for Seth to answer me.

My eyes flick from the black screen back to Cami as I turn it on and wait, but there's no response.

Heaving in a breath, I have to use the cold wall to stand upright, but my legs are too shaky. That's when the tears start again. Heavy, hard sobs.

She's dead.

This life costs more than I'm willing to give.

My inhale is shaky until I hear a bump outside. I freeze, even with dizzy vision, I go stone-still. I've been here long enough for whoever did this to her to come get me if they wanted. Maybe they wanted to see my heart shatter before they killed me too.

Silence, followed by more silence. It was something crashing against the house. I know I heard it.

Thump. Again I hear the sound and this time it's accompanied by the muted howl of the night wind. It's just the trash can hitting the back of the house.

It's just the trash can hitting the back of the house. I tell myself again, hoping it will calm me down but it doesn't. The wind screams and the plastic can bangs against the back of the house again.

With my eyes closed, I breathe in and out. It's okay. I'm okay.

"Please answer me, Seth." I whisper the words, only to open my eyes and see no response and Cami's dead body on the floor.

Her skin is so pale.

It takes everything in me to lean down. Even as bile rises in the back of my throat, I carry through with it, hot tears streaming down my cheeks. It's easier to close her eyes than I thought it would be. Her thick lashes feel wet beneath my fingers and I don't know if it's from my clammy hands or tears that had gathered there.

I don't say goodbye to her, but I know it's the last time I'll see her when I lift my hand and her eyes are closed.

My steps are hurried and loud as I make my way to the bathroom, turning the faucet up as hot as it'll go and viciously rubbing my hands clean.

It's too loud. The water is so loud I can't hear anything that could be going on around me, so I'm quick to shut it off even though I don't feel clean enough.

My back hits the bathroom wall as I stand there, staring at myself in the mirror. Disheveled hair, wild eyes, and hot pink cheeks. It's obvious I've been crying. It's obvious I'm lost.

It's obvious I can't stay here.

I have nowhere else to go, though. Nowhere around here is safe. I'm not safe. Jackson was right. I have to save myself.

Time slows as the next thoughts come to me. The clicks of the ever-present clock seeming to tick longer with pauses between each one, punctuating each moment of clarity.

The money is in the safe. A safe that couldn't be opened by Cami because she didn't know the code. That's why they tied her up. They wanted the code; they wanted the money.

Tick.

The money they killed her trying to get.

Tock.

The money meant for a better life according to Seth, and it cost my best friend her last breath.

Tick.

Money Seth will use for guns, drugs, gambling.

Tock.

Money I need to get the hell out of here.

Tick.

It's over just like that.

Maybe five seconds have passed. But it feels like an eternity. It feels like the weight of the world. It feels like the end.

I'm still shaking when I hear the rapid beeps as I enter the code into the keypad. The click of the lock unlatching and the ease with which the heavy metal door opens only brings a new pain.

If only I had told Cami the code.

If I could go back in time and tell it to her, let it slide that the code was our anniversary date, I would have even though she never would have asked. Maybe she would have been in less pain. Maybe it would have been faster if she could have just told them the code.

With cloudy vision, I try to shut down the visuals of what happened to her hours ago.

I don't know how much money is here. I've never asked and I don't count now.

There are stacks and stacks of cash neatly arranged into bundles that are easy to grab by the fistful. I have to back away for a moment, questioning myself but the question is gone as quickly as it came.

I can't wait for next time.

I can't keep going like this.

There's a backpack, one I'd planned to take to nursing school if I ever got into one, in the far corner of the closet. I know it's there and the memory of it forces me to move quickly on these insecure legs. I unzip it on my way back to the safe, and dump its contents, unused notebooks and packs of pens, onto the safe floor.

I take a stack of cash and then another.

I have my car, money, and enough fear to push me far away from here.

Seth's face is there every time I close my eyes. The hurt, the disappointment. Picturing his sad eyes makes me waver, but only enough that I pause. I don't stop packing.

I've begged him. I've told him I can't stay.

Another stack and the backpack is full. It's six large stacks in total and a little more than a quarter of what was in here.

I have trouble zipping it up. The little metal zipper slips from my fingers and then snags on the bills the next time I try.

I'm a hell of a mess. Scared and damaged. In raw pain from losing Cami, but also from knowing how I'm leaving Seth right now.

I won't wait for him anymore. With that thought, I shut the safe door, leaning my back against it as I heave in oxygen, praying for it to calm me down enough to drive away. I'm faster packing a bag, grabbing everything I can without bothering to remove the hangers. I shove it all in, eager to get the hell out of here.

A small voice whispers to wait. It begs me to check my phone again, to give Seth one more chance.

Oh, how my body bends to that will. I wish he would have texted. I wish he would have been waiting for me right then and there. To stop me from going alone. I want him to come with me.

I need him to. Or in this last moment of weakness, to force me to stay. I wish he were here now to shove me in the safe, like he said he would. Because I don't want to leave. Even now, I'm so aware I don't want to leave.

But Seth isn't here. He didn't text me back. And he isn't going to leave this life. He'll never leave it.

This life is who he is. I know that it is.

My swallow is harsh and ragged, like broken glass slicing its way down when I get to the front door.

My hands are so cold now, they're numb. My entire body is by this point.

I stare at the red door, envisioning Seth walking through it. I wait for one beat of my heart and then it's followed by another fucked-up beat that skips all over. But he doesn't come.

I would have been dead for hours and hours, and then what? What would he do "next time?"

The bookbag drops to the tile floor with a thud as I walk around the counter, pull out the junk drawer in the kitchen and grab a small pad of paper and a pen.

I have to scribble the pen for a moment to get the ink flowing, so I move to the second sheet. Letting the tears flow, I take out another clean sheet to write down my last words to him.

He'll never forgive me. I already know that.

I don't think I'll ever forgive myself either.

The clean sheet is stained by a fallen tear before the tip of the pen can mar the perfectly white paper with a slash of black.

I'll always love you.

I write that line first but the others aren't good enough. *Please forgive me.* I think that thought every other line, but I never write it. *I had to.* I don't have to, I'm choosing to and I know it. He knows it too.

The only truth I can bear to give him is that I'll always love him.

Then I write my final thought.

Even if you hate me, I'll always love you.

There can't be any blood in my hands or face; they're cold and numb. I know that much from the pricks that travel along my icy flesh. It's all drained from me. I don't know how long I stand there, wishing for better words that don't come.

Wishing it wasn't over, but knowing that it is.

It's over.

I'm leaving him.

The resolution gives me enough strength to move, but I still linger at the door, gripping the edge of it as I whisper, "I'm sorry, babe," to Cami. "I love you."

I think about her as I wipe my face and drive away in the dark night. The headlights shine ahead of me, two yellow streaks in a sea of nothing.

It's my fault. I knew who Seth was, I just never thought that there wouldn't be a way for our lives to fit together. It was always so perfect, so easy. He was my everything.

Occasionally I glance at the backpack in the passenger seat, the money I stole from him. When I get to a motel hours and hours away with sleep dragging me down, I finally check my phone for the first time since I left.

There's nothing from him. Nothing after the texts I sent him to come home and that I wasn't okay. He saw them though. He saw but he didn't answer.

Derrick messaged me, though. Reading his text sends me into another sobbing frenzy on the scratchy sheets of the motel.

Tonight is the first night of many where I simply cry myself to sleep, hating who I am and how little I'm worth. And it's the first night in years that Seth doesn't message me back. He never messages me back.

CHAPTER 19

Seth

FUCK.

"No, no, no." With my hands running down my face I keep praying to whatever God would even bother to listen to me to make Cami wake up. To make this entire night go away. Erase it from fate's plans. None of this should have happened.

"Please, God," I beg, but no one's listening to me.

Derrick hasn't moved. Not an inch. His body is over Cami's, his forearm resting above her head. His face is near her stomach, and his shoulders heave every so often. I've never seen the man cry in our entire existence, but he cries for her.

"We're too late," I tell him again, with a dry throat and hope he hears me this time. My fist slams against the wall when he tells me "no" like this isn't real. The pain of my knuckles bashing against the wall isn't enough. The pain is miniscule compared to everything else. So I do it again and again, letting the anguish wash over me. The drywall cracks and crumbles so easily.

I don't even realize I'm screaming until Derrick yells at me to shut the fuck up.

Picking up his head, he stares at me, both of us breathless, wounded and guilty.

"This is because of me," he tells me with red eyes. The pain is etched in every feature of his expression. "She's dead because I couldn't—"

"She's dead because Mathews wanted to hurt us. They wanted to steal from us. They wanted to kill her."

"It's on me," he emphasizes, lowering himself until his forehead rests on her stomach. "She died because of me."

"We'll get them back. We'll make them pay."

Time passes in silence.

"Where's Laura?" he asks cautiously. He didn't see the note when we came in. It's the first thing I saw. The blood, the trail of it to the safe. The emptied backpack.

"She took off," I answer him and I swear the confession strangles me. Each word tries to choke me, hating the very thought of it.

"Where she'd run to?" he asks and the lack of contempt, the lack of sympathy… he doesn't get it.

"She didn't run from them; she took off for good," I explain. It hurts more than I thought it would to say it out loud. "She left me."

With bewildered eyes he shakes his head and that's when I turn away from him, leaving him where he is over Cami and walking away. I have to wipe my face with my forearm as I head back to the kitchen and to the front of the house.

I feel restless, anxious, tormented and angry. It turns to pacing, thinking about how to get revenge against Mathews for hurting Laura, for trying to steal from me, for scaring the one girl I've ever loved away from me.

I can picture Laura finding Cami; that breaks me down to nothing. I am nothing when I imagine that scene. I know how she would have reacted. But I can't see her emptying the backpack and shoving the money inside. I can't see her packing up her things. I can't picture her leaving me.

Never did I think she'd leave me. I can't imagine it, even though it's already done.

The ghosts in the living room call to me. She wanted me to leave. I did this. I did all of this.

Another vicious scream tears from my throat as I swipe my arm down the counter. My body's hot, my head feels light and I do it again. The bang and clatter of the broken glasses and pans hitting the tiled floor urge me on.

I destroy everything, everything I touch, why should this place be any different?

It takes me a long moment to realize she took the cash and what the consequence of that is. I needed that cash. We needed every fucking cent of it.

"Fuck!" I scream out the word, but it doesn't make anything better.

This is what it feels like to be at rock bottom.

It takes a long time for me to actually cry. To let it all out and feel the deep-seated pain in the very pit of my stomach. For me to accept that Cami is dead and Laura is long gone.

Getting revenge for Cami is the sole focus of our crew.

That's the only thing that keeps Derrick moving. The guys are silent. Everyone is. No one asks where Laura is either. They know she left; they don't know about the money though.

If I told them, they'd want to go after her. So instead I have to be smarter, harsher, more violent to get the message across.

She screwed me. Laura screwed me over when she left. She left me at my worst, and made everything harder. I have to tell myself she couldn't have known, but that only helps for so long.

It takes hours of standing in a scalding hot shower to try to wash it all away, the pain of what I've caused, the agony of what I lost. It doesn't leave me though. There's no cleansing these sins.

When I fall into bed, I take her note with me. It crinkles when I grip it, no matter how much I try to let up on my grasp. I can't help it; I hold it with everything I've got.

I have her note, and the messages she sent.

The dim light from the phone is the only light in the room, and I stare at it for hours. Reading the texts about her doctor's appointment, then about Cami. I reread the lines she sent, wanting me to come home. Needing me.

Instead I was out, making a hard life even harder. Getting us into deeper shit.

All the while she was dealing with a dead girl whose blood is on my hands.

There's a mix of regret and hate.

As the weeks move on, I get colder, harder. The realization of what I've chosen fuels me to do unspeakable things. Mathews never stood a chance. Neither did Fletcher.

Laura doesn't text me again other than to tell me she's sorry and I don't respond to that message. She doesn't come back to Tremont or anywhere within a five-hundred-mile radius. Well only once, and it wasn't for me. A year had passed and she came back for a single day, hoping not to run into me even though she stepped into my territory, into my bar. I knew it when she saw me there, bumping into me by accident, that she wanted to leave without running into me.

That hurt stays long after she's gone. I thought I wasn't capable of feeling like that anymore, until she showed up.

Derrick keeps tabs on her. He has since she left.

The regret fades. The hate takes over.

I loved her more than she loved me, because I never would have left her.

Every day that passes, I start hating her more.

She said she loved me and she left.

She stole from me and she left.

She never looked back; she just left.

She should have known one day I'd come back for her. I'm going to make her feel the same regret I feel.

◎

Eight years later

I wonder if Laura knows it's me, for about half a fucking second. The way she averts her eyes and refuses to look at me gives me the answer I'm looking for. The East Coast has been good to me. I wouldn't have chosen it for myself, but it's where Laura ended up.

It's pitch black and the stores in the shopping center are closing down. I've been parked here for a good three hours now, just watching. It's what I'm paid to do and what I need to do tonight.

I'm supposed to watch Jase Cross's girl. I've been working with the Cross brothers ever since I left Tremont in Derrick's hands. There was no one left to kill there, no challenges to face. So I followed Laura, keeping my distance and getting comfortable.

Fate's a prick.

She's with the girl I'm supposed to be keeping an eye on. I suppose it makes sense. My life's a sick joke.

Fuck, just looking at her dredges up everything. Every splinter of emotion I thought I'd long buried. The sick concoction of it all slips into the crevices of my bones as my eyes wander over the curves of her collarbone.

Then lower, to the dip at her waist.

It's hot and cold. Anger then lust. Fuck, I can't keep still in this piece of tin knowing she's right there. So damn close, I could go get her if only I wanted to. Some moments I do, but I don't know that I'm ready yet and I need her to come to me. A piece of me *needs* her to be the one to come to me.

Her eyes catch mine once, then twice. She turns stiff in the car across the vacant parking lot.

I bet she thinks I'm here for her. She thinks this is about her, and maybe it was when I first moved here. Now though, I have plenty to keep myself occupied here before I attend to her.

If she thinks what's between us is over, she's wrong.

If she thinks I'm going to let her get away with it, she's out of her fucking mind.

The wine bottle is nearly empty in her hands as she sits in the driver's seat. I've been watching her and Bethany, Jase's girl, drink at the bar, go into a shop, drink at another bar, and go into another shop all damn night. They're both on the verge of fucked up when Bethany knocks on my window, wanting a ride.

The slow smirk is hard to hide when I roll down my window. She thinks she can trust me. She hasn't learned that in this life, you can't trust anyone. Not even the ones you love.

Bethany's a sweet girl but oblivious. It's nearly sick how much I revel in her unsuspecting question to simply take them home.

Bethany gets in easily enough, feeling safe and secure because she knows her boyfriend is my boss. She knows I won't do a damn thing to hurt her.

She has no idea what I want to do to Laura, though. She isn't aware that I know her. I know Laura more than I know anyone.

The click of Laura's car door echoes in the empty lot as does the staccato of her heels as she makes her way to my car. I remember those blue eyes spearing into mine when she peeks at me through her thick lashes.

She gets in without a word, but the air burns hot. Her friend is clueless. Utterly unaware.

I can't hear a damn word Bethany's saying of the confession that spills from her and I wonder if Laura can hear it. If she has the patience for it, the mental capacity to think of anything other than what I'm going to do to her once Bethany gets her ass out of this car.

The few miles it takes to drop off Bethany are far too long. Every second is drawn out by the deep breaths Laura takes.

My grip tightens on the wheel, thinning the tight skin on my knuckles and turning it white. The click of the turn signal distracts me from whatever Bethany's saying, but not from the sweet cadence of Laura's response.

Her voice is a memory that thickens the tension between us.

It takes fifteen minutes until Bethany's out of the car, closing the door and asking me sweetly to take Laura home.

I've been in this town for years now. I've come close to seeing the girl who stole my heart and left me with nothing, face to face, more times than I can count. I've been patient though. *Good things come to those who wait.*

It's not until Bethany closes the front door, that Laura speaks to me.

"Seth." Laura speaks my name like a sin. She has to clear her throat after she says my name, the nerves eating away at her and showing easily enough.

The leather groans in the back of my car as she adjusts in her seat.

I'm already down the pebbled path of the driveway, minutes from the highway and debating on which way I should go. Left to her place, or right, to mine.

"Seth, please," she begs me although I don't know what for.

I'm silent, remembering all the times she begged me before when she was under me, writhing and loving me.

I love you. How many times did she tell me that just minutes after moaning my name like she used to do?

I can hear her swallow and in the rearview mirror, I watch as her chest rises and falls heavier with each passing second that I don't acknowledge her.

"Seth, would you say something please, you're scaring me."

Scaring her? If she knew what I became when she left me, she'd be fucking terrified.

My gaze moves to the mirror, watching her nervously bite down on her lower lip. Those plump lips I used to bite myself.

Licking my own, I let out a deep sigh and sit back into my seat, easing the tense muscles and letting more time pass simply to torture her.

She leans forward, refusing to just wait like a good girl. Her hand grips the top of my seat, her fingers brushing my shoulder. The short touch is gentle, seemingly innocuous, but it lights up every nerve ending in me.

"Seth, please, just talk to me." As she speaks, her voice cracks and her eyes turn glossy.

I can feel how her heart breaks only inches from mine. Her pain is like a hit of ecstasy after years of being clean. I want more of it; I crave it like an addict.

"What do you want me to say, Babygirl?" I question her and wait at the red light, right at the fork that decides where we're going.

I can hear the hitch in her breath, I can feel the heat that revs up inside of her. Was it *Babygirl* that did it? Or simply having me answer her after nearly a decade of silence?

Inhaling deeply, I get a heavy dose of her sweet scent. Fuck, it's just like I remember. Everything about her is exactly what I remember. I didn't make it up in my mind. She's intoxicating.

"Anything," she breathes as the red light turns green and I make my decision, knowing exactly what I'm going to do to her tonight, how I'm going to make her pay for leaving me and fucking me over. "Just tell me anything."

ABOUT THE AUTHOR

Thank you so much for reading my romances. I'm just a stay at home mom and avid reader turned author and I couldn't be happier.

I hope you love my books as much as I do!

More by Willow Winters
www.willowwinterswrites.com/books

Locking my gaze with hers I ask her, keeping my voice low to try to hide the anger, "How did you really think this was going to end?"